Aisha licked her lips as she thought about how smooth and agile Patrick had been playing that dance game

He hadn't lied at all. He certainly had moves. She wondered what other kind of moves he had, and she licked her lips again.

This time without any warning or announcement, Patrick swooped down and covered her lips with his. And this wasn't one of those soft, fleeting brushes he'd been priming her up with. No, this was a long, savoring, enveloping kiss.

She opened to his demanding mouth and let her tongue taste what it really wanted to taste. Him. He pulled her off the sofa and onto his lap, continuing to devour her with his scalding-hot mouth. She had started something that he was clearly going to finish.

Aisha felt overwhelmed. She had never had a man be so attentive to her needs. She started to glimpse the gentle soul that was hiding behind the domineering persona and began to fear that she was already losing her heart to him. When Patrick kissed her again, she knew for sure that it was already gone.

Books by Gwyneth Bolton

Kimani Romance

If Only You Knew
Protect and Serve
Make It Hot
The Law of Desire
Sizzling Seduction

GWYNETH BOLTON

was born and raised in Paterson, New Jersey. She currently lives in central New York with her husband, Cedric. When she was twelve years old she became an avid reader of romance by sneaking into her mother's stash of Harlequin and Silhouette novels. In the '90s she was introduced to African-American and multicultural romance novels and her life hasn't been the same since.

Bolton has a BA and an MA in English/creative writing and a PhD in English/composition and rhetoric. She teaches classes in writing and women's studies at the college level. She has won several awards for her romance novels, including five Emma Awards and a Romance in Color Reviewer's Choice award for new author of the year. When she is not teaching or working on her own romance novels, she is curled up with a cup of herbal tea, a warm quilt and a good book. She can be reached via e-mail at gwynethbolton@prodigy.net, and readers can also visit her Web site, www.gwynethbolton.com.

SIZZLING
SEDUCTION

Gwyneth Bolton

To the readers…

Thanks for writing me and telling me that you enjoyed the Hightowers. And thanks for helping to spread the word about the series. I appreciate you all very much. I am because you are. Thank you!

 KIMANI PRESS™

ISBN-13: 978-0-373-86134-7

SIZZLING SEDUCTION

Copyright © 2009 by Gwendolyn Pough.

www.kimanipress.com

Printed in U.S.A.

Dear Reader,

Thank you so much for your support of the Hightower Honors series. There are really no words to properly express how much your e-mails and notes have meant to me. I'm happy that so many of you have fallen in love with this family as much as I have. And for those readers who read the earlier novels and decided that Patrick Hightower was the one for them, here he is!

We all know Patrick was the president of the he-man woman-haters club. He is the oldest Hightower brother and the most resistant to love. So you know once love caught up to him, Cupid had to knock him off his feet hard and fast. Too bad he ends up falling for a woman just as resistant to falling in love as he had been!

Aisha Miller is the perfect woman for Patrick, but the divorced mother and kindergarten teacher refuses to acknowledge it. It's up to Patrick to pull out all the stops and seduce the woman of his dreams right into his arms.

Sizzling Seduction is a slow-burning love story that steadily rises to an uncontrollable, passionate heat. It is a story about trust and learning to love again.

I hope you enjoy Patrick and Aisha's story!

Gwyneth

ACKNOWLEDGMENTS

First, I want to thank God for the many blessings in my life.

I'd also like to thank the following people because they were so instrumental in my getting the Hightower firemen right: Kristi Johnson, Wayne Rochette and Lieutenant Kent Young. All three of these people are part of that special team who help to protect and serve. Kristi, a volunteer EMT, and her partner Wayne Rochette, a volunteer firefighter, helped me to flesh out Joel Hightower's motivation back when I wrote *Make It Hot.* My editor wanted me to dig deeper and really get into Joel's head about why he loved being a firefighter. Kristi and Wayne provided the perfect insight! Kristi was then kind enough to bug Wayne one more time and they put me in contact with Lieutenant Kent Young of Fire Station Five in Syracuse. Lieutenant Young took time out of his busy schedule to talk to me about the job and give me a tour of the station. He also gave me the coolest coloring book they give to schoolchildren who visit the station. *Syracuse Fire Department Presents Fire Safety with Helpful Hector the Smoke Detector and Buddy the Battery* gave me the perfect inspiration for the initial meeting scene between Patrick and Aisha when she visits the fire station with her kindergarteners. Lieutenant Young's comments and tour helped me to really flesh out what Patrick's day might be like. Any mistakes or misrepresentations of the firefighting life are mine and mine alone.

Finally, I'd like to thank my family: my mother, Donna, my sisters Jennifer, Cassandra, Michelle and Tashina, my nieces Ashlee and Zaria, and my husband, Cedric.

Chapter 1

"Rise and shine, Dillon. Time to get up and get dressed for school. Regular oatmeal or cream of wheat?" Aisha Miller stood in the doorway of her ten-year-old son's Spider-Man–decorated room and started their morning ritual. She knew that she would probably have to make at least one more trip back there before he dragged himself from bed.

He made an indistinguishable groaning sound, but he didn't move.

"Dillon, don't make me have to come in there. Get up. We don't want to be late. I'm going to start the oatmeal. By the time it's done and I come back here again, you better be washed up and getting dressed. Your clothes are on the chair."

He made another groaning sound. But this time he moved and sat up, pulling the Spider-Man sheets from over his head. "Cap'n Crunch," he uttered before flopping back down.

Instead of the bargaining-for-more-time-to-sleep battle he was starting with the bargaining-for-sweets-to-eat battle. Aisha grinned. Her son certainly kept her on her toes.

"Cream of wheat," she countered.

He got up from bed and did a slow-dragging walk to the bathroom. "Corn Pops."

"Umm…no… Oatmeal or cream of wheat?"

He gave a resigned sigh. "Cream of wheat."

"Okay, get washed up and dressed. We need to be out the door before seven-thirty. I'm taking my morning class on a trip to the fire station today and I need to get to school a little early in order to handle some paperwork. Paperwork that needs to be turned in to Principal Gibson today. So stop dragging those little feet and let's get rolling."

He groaned again and half dragged on down the hall. She couldn't help but chuckle. He reminded her so much of herself when she was a kid. She'd never liked getting up in the morning for school and always tried to negotiate with her mother for an extra five minutes. In fact, if she didn't have to get both herself and Dillon ready, she would have hit the snooze button a few times and would just be crawling out of bed herself.

When she got the cream of wheat going she took a trip back down the hall and saw that Dillon had made it to the living room and was watching morning cartoons while he put on his clothing. Really, he was staring at the screen and punctuating the long stretches of viewing by placing one item of clothing on his body at a time. At the rate he was going, he'd be dressed by the time the afternoon talk shows came on.

She walked over and turned off the television. "This is why you don't have a television in your bedroom, Dillon. And what did I tell you about coming in here and turning on the television before you get dressed? If you got up on time and got dressed quickly, you'd have a couple of minutes to catch some cartoons before it was time to go."

"Aw-ww…Mo-m…"

"Don't aww mom me. Hurry up before your breakfast gets cold."

Dillon moved considerably faster without the distraction of the television and soon he was fed and they were out the door, in the car and on their way.

"I have the coolest idea, Mom." Dillon literally bounced with excitement in the passenger seat.

"Really, I can't wait to hear it. What's your cool idea?"

"You can write my teacher a note and take me to the fire station with your class today. That would be so cool. I've never been to a real fire station. I wonder if they'd let me slide down the pole?"

"I can tell you the answer to that. They wouldn't because you won't be going to the fire station. You can't miss class to go on someone else's trip. And you wouldn't want to hang out with my little darling kindergartners."

Dillon got a pensive expression on his face as if he was considering the merits of getting out of school versus spending the morning with kindergartners. He frowned. "Well, it seemed like it might have been a cool idea. But now that I think about it…"

"Mmm-hmm…" She pulled into the parking lot. Before getting out she leaned over and offered her cheek to her son. He had reached the age where any public displays of affection from Mom would embarrass him to no end. So she always made sure to get her sugar before they got out of the car.

Dillon offered only one "Awww, Mom" before giving her a quick peck on the cheek and dashing out of the car to the school building.

She got out, grabbed her bags and supplies and followed closely behind. "And you stop that running once you get in the building. You don't want Principal Gibson to give you detention."

"Okay, Mom." Dillon slowed his pace when he reached the big blue doors of Public School #21. He pulled the door open and held it for her as she walked in.

"Thank you, sweetie."

"M-ooo-m. No 'sweetie' in school—somebody might hear you."

She laughed. "Keep it up and I'm going to give to give you a big hug in front of all your friends."

She watched her son walk up to the second floor of the building for his before-school math tutoring. Ms. McCloud was kind enough to see him before school to help him with his math.

The building was still somewhat quiet. But soon it would be bustling with the sounds of children learning and playing. PS #21 was a kindergarten through eighth grade elementary school in the heart of Paterson, New Jersey, on Tenth Avenue. She'd been lucky to get a job teaching in the same school district in which she lived, at the school closest to her home and the one her son attended. Dillon probably didn't think so, but it worked for her.

Once she'd finished her paperwork and returned from the principal's office, her teacher's assistant, Toni, had arrived.

Aisha smiled. "Well, well, look who's on time today."

Toni grinned and waved her off. "Girl, please, of course I'm on time today. I can't wait to take these little rug rats to the fire station. My future husband might be waiting for me as we speak. I can't keep my hunky fireman husband-to-be waiting. How do I look?" Toni did a little spin and showed off her latest trendy outfit. The bold splash of orange and purple in the blouse refused to be outdone by the orange skirt, dark plum tights and purple patent-leather boots. But with Toni's wild personality the outfit worked.

Aisha knew she could never pull off something like that—not that she would have any desire to. Just give her a pair of neutral slacks and a nice sweater twinset any day. Maybe some gold jewelry.

"You look…nice…" Aisha started. Toni really did look nice—not Aisha's personal taste, but nice nonetheless.

Toni cut her eyes. "You don't like the outfit. I can tell. But my future fireman husband is going to be all on it. You watch and see. Plus, everyone can't pull off prissy-priss-chic like you. Some of us need flair."

"Prissy-priss?" Aisha feigned indignation. "That's Ms. Priss, thank you very much. I can't help it if I'm a little more reserved.…"

"Ummm… Reserved isn't going to snag you one of those hot firemen. You'll see. Watch me work it, girl." Toni did a little spin and shook her head so that the blunt edges of her stylish haircut moved with sassy precision.

Aisha just laughed. She wasn't looking for a hot, sexy fireman as a future husband, boyfriend or anything else. The only man she had time for in her life was ten years old and upstairs being tutored in math. Being Dillon's mom and being the best kindergarten teacher she could be was more than enough for her.

One by one the students started showing up, and soon she had an entire classroom full of kiddies. After a brief morning lesson, they'd take the six-block walk to Fire Station No. 5 and get a tour and a lesson in fire safety.

Aisha grinned in anticipation. She liked taking class trips almost as much as the kids did. She couldn't wait.

Patrick Hightower eyed his squad as they lined up in the apparatus room for roll call. Of the five men on duty on any given shift, his position as fire captain never changed.

He was the officer in charge.

He took note of his men. All of them were present and accounted for, uniformed and ready to roll at the sound of an alarm. Reggie Smith, the rookie, was there and Patrick had a special assignment for him today. They had a group of kindergartners coming through later, and the rookie could give them a tour.

"Jones, you're the driver today." Patrick went down his list. "Carter, you're position three. Stone, you're position four. And Smith, you're position five, waterman and general helper."

"No big surprise there," Reggie grumbled.

"Awww…the rookie's getting tired of playing his position." Lennie Stone playfully ribbed Reggie.

The other men laughed, and Patrick was tempted to join them. But he had one more surprise for the rookie. Holding back his own grin, he added, "And we have a tour today. So you can show us what you know, rookie, by leading the tour and giving a presentation to the group of kindergarteners we have coming in."

"Kindergartners?" A look of horror crossed Reggie's face. "Couldn't my first time leading a tour be with some older kids? The small ones scare me." Reggie offered a fake shiver.

"Hey, if you can face a fire you can face some five-year-olds," Patrick said.

"I don't know. I think I'd take my chances with the fire anytime." Bryan Carter winked, shaking his head in mock sympathy.

Patrick went over the rest of the schedule for the day, knowing that one call would set his entire carefully planned schedule off for the day. Once he set out the schedule, the men went about checking the fire engine and equipment to make sure that everything was fully operational.

There were two other firefighters who were also certified first-responder and emergency medical technicians on this shift besides himself, and Patrick knew that the men would also check the medical equipment and verify that all medications were there.

Patrick went back to his office/bedroom to log personnel and equipment on to the computer and wrap up a few other administrative ends.

The room that he spent more time in than he spent in his own bedroom at home housed a desk, a twin bed, a couple of chairs, a computer and printer. The décor probably left a lot to be desired for most folks. The beige-and-brown comforter on the bed and the cream plaid chairs didn't exactly scream high-end. But it was sufficient for the work he needed to get done.

His cell phone started ringing and he glanced at the caller ID before answering.

"Yes, Aunt Sophie?"

"How's my favorite nephew this morning?" Her voice was way too pleasant for the time of morning and for her demeanor in general.

Something was up. She was that pleasant only when she was trying to hook him up with some woman she thought would be perfect for him.

Been there, done that and got the divorce papers to prove it.

There was no way he was going to allow her to reel him in and hook him up. Plus, if he weren't at work it would be too early for his aunt to be calling him anyway. She must be trying to catch him when he was sleepy and groggy and liable to agree to anything.

"I'm fine, Aunt Sophie. But I'm at work and I can't talk now. I need to run the guys through a drill and we have to handle chores at the station before a group of kids come through for a tour in a few." He almost felt guilty rushing her off the phone. Almost. "So how about I give you a call later this week? In fact, I'll try and make time to take my favorite aunt out to lunch. Okay? I really have to go now."

"Well…okay…I guess I can run some things by you over lunch. I just think you've been single too long and it's time for you to just—"

"Yeah, this is definitely a lunchtime conversation." *Not.* "I'll give you a call later this week and we can set up a time. Love you, Aunt Sophie. I'll talk with you later. Bye-bye."

"Well…fine…bye, Patrick. We will talk later—I have some ideas. I'm concerned about your happiness. I don't think you've ever gotten over Courtney. And—"

"Sorry, gotta run, Aunt Sophie. I'll call you. Bye."

Yeah, he had to cut her off before she went there. Bringing up the ex-wife was a good enough reason for the dial tone. Sophie was lucky he had respect for his elders. He hung up the phone. The last thing he needed this early in the morning was a reminder of the biggest mistake of his life.

Shaking his head, he got up and started the drill exercise for the morning. They had just enough time to run through it before the kiddies came through.

People had these outrageous images of firemen just sitting around the firehouse playing cards and dominoes and waiting for the alarm to ring. Those images went out with Ward and Beaver. Today's firemen were constantly learning and growing on the job, with multiple drills performed daily, as well as video training and lectures. They also had to clean the firehouse, cook and perform community outreach by going to schools and offering tours to students. The job was multifaceted and he loved that part of it, almost as much as he loved running into a blaze and saving lives.

He put the team through a drill of working the hose while on the ladder. And soon the little ones were coming through the door. He fully intended to greet them and then get the heck out of Dodge.

"Welcome to Fire Station No. 5, girls and boys. My name is Fire Captain Patrick Hightower." He paused and gave them a chance to settle down a little. They were clearly hyped from the walk over, and some of them seemed literally ready to bounce off the walls. He scanned the crowd of munchkins, then sought out their teacher.

Good, he thought; there are two of them. They should be able to keep the kids corralled. His eyes skimmed right over the young woman with the weird boots, even though she did look familiar. Did she go to his church? She seemed to be striking a pose as if she was waiting to be noticed or something.

The other teacher was bent over, consoling a little girl who had apparently tripped coming into the building. He zeroed in on her behind and chastised himself even as he checked her out. A backside like that deserved more than a passing glance, but he knew it wasn't the time or the place.

She was good with the little kid, though. She seemed to have the right amount of patience and kindness needed to deal with kids at such a tender age. The little girl seemed more embarrassed than actually hurt. But the teacher treated the child as if she were the center of the universe. And soon the little girl was cracking a snaggle-toothed grin.

The teacher stood up. "Sorry about that, Captain…." Her voice trailed off as she caught his gaze. The most beautiful brown eyes he'd ever seen caught his eyes and held them.

He opened his mouth and closed it several times. The little ones had long since settled down, and they were looking at him expectantly.

She was stunning.

He stared. He couldn't help it. And apparently neither could she, because she just kept looking at him as if she couldn't pull her gaze away.

He cleared his throat, still keeping his focus on her. "As I said, welcome to Fire Station No. 5. I'm Captain Patrick Hightower and I'm going to leave you in the very capable hands of Firefighter Reggie Smith. He'll

be guiding your tour today and answering all of your
questions. Enjoy yourselves."

He should have left and gone back to his office then.
But he couldn't. He just couldn't.

Chapter 2

As many times as Patrick had given the welcoming spiel, as many times as he had handed over the reins of the student visits to the firehouse to some poor rookie who had the pleasure of leading the schoolchildren on their tour, Patrick couldn't figure out why he couldn't move his legs. And what in the hell was wrong with his tongue?

He looked her up and down. She came to about his shoulder and had a curvy body, skin that was a rich shade of brown with reddish undertones, and wore her long, brown hair away from her face with a dark blue headband. Her eyes looked as if someone had taken canes of light and dark brown sugar and spun them together. Yes, she was sugar and spice and everything nice…

Staring at the woman, who made navy blue slacks, a powder-blue sweater twinset, pearl earrings and a necklace look like one of Victoria's deepest, most scintillating secrets, he realized the kindergarten teacher had something to do with his sudden speechlessness. Patrick had always been good at warding off any chance of having his heart stolen again.

He just didn't know how it managed to happen, and how he never had a chance to stop it. But if the erratic thumping in his chest and the sudden clamminess in his hands were any indication, he was smitten with the sexy schoolteacher.

Oh, he didn't have a problem with the opposite sex, per se. He just has a problem with being so taken by a woman he couldn't move or speak. Short, hot, steamy affairs he could do and do again. But this…

This was new. This was dangerous. This was worse than running headfirst into a five-alarm blaze with no gear and no clue. And this…

This was inevitable.

At the age of forty, after thinking he would dodge this ever happening to him again, Patrick Hightower had just met a woman he actually wanted to get to know better.

Some men just take up all the space and air in the room. And given that fact, Aisha Miller sized him up.

Tall, dark and handsome had nothing on this towering wall of muscles or the way he filled out that navy blue-and-white uniform. She didn't think she had a thing for men in uniform. Thick, muscular thighs, strong pipes for arms, official and authoritative clothing…her heart raced.

She tried to focus on other things in the firehouse. *The truck? Look at it—all red and shiny and pretty. The engine…*

Just listen to the words. Focus on the words. Focus on my students. Ignore this man.

As if she could…

"Stay away from hot things that can hurt!" Her kindergarten students yelled the words at the top of their little lungs as they repeated after the young fireman who had just given them a tour of the fire station.

Their guide was in his early twenties and seemed to be having just as much fun as the kids. He didn't look bad in his uniform, either. Maybe she could try to focus on him.

Nope, even the cute little tender-roni fireman guide couldn't distract her.

She glanced at Toni in her outrageous purple-and-orange getup trying to catch the young firefighter's eye by flirtingly repeating after him with the children. Surely Toni's antics should have wrestled her attention from the sexy fire captain. Toni batted her eyes, and Aisha's eyes went right back to the fire captain.

Dang!

Aisha couldn't help it. She stared at the sexy, very hot fire captain who was standing there watching them all. Captain Hightower. He'd said his name was Captain Patrick Hightower. She wondered why he was still in the room. He wasn't giving them the tour. Last year when she'd brought her students for a tour, the highest-ranking officer on duty had introduced himself, given them a welcome and hightailed it out of there, leaving it up to the young rookie to do the grunt work.

Tall. Rock-hard. Solid muscle and masculinity. Devil-may-care smile. *Oh, yeah.* He was a hot thing that could hurt all right.

"Tell a grown-up when you find matches or lighters," the students yelled.

"Stop, drop and roll if your clothes catch on fire." They dropped on the ground and rolled around.

"Cool a burn!" Their little voices piped through the huge hall.

"That's right. If you happen to burn yourselves, you should immediately cover the spot with cold water." The rookie firefighter whose name she *still* could not remember—as if she could remember another name with the name *Patrick Hightower* taking over every nook and crevice of her mind—coached the children with gems of fire safety.

Cold water would have been good at that moment. It might have helped with the sudden heat she was feeling. She could drink a glass and cool her dry-as-the-desert mouth and throat. She could splash it all over herself to calm down the overwhelming body heat she felt when she looked at Patrick Hightower. The heat and the sweat popping out all over her was unbearable.

Early menopause? It could happen as early as thirty-five. She was thirty-five. But something told her it wasn't early menopause causing the steam to roll up her neck and making her hand want to fan, fan and fan away.

"Crawl low under smoke!" her little darlings repeated.

"Know the sound of the smoke alarm," they added.

The ringing of the alarm jolted her and she blinked.

Sound effects? Hmm... She certainly needed a warning if Captain Hightower's heated stare meant what she thought it meant.

"Practice an escape plan," the kindergarteners said with the same tone of authority that the young rookie had used.

You haven't said anything but a word!

She needed an escape plan. She took a slow, calming and deep breath and tried to appear natural about letting it out. No matter what, she wasn't going to give the man the time of day. That was for sure. She couldn't. She wouldn't. So there was really no need to get all nervous and hot and bothered.

"Recognize the firefighter as a helper," the children chanted after the rookie.

Yeah.

Right.

She glanced up at the fire captain again. He smiled, a sexy, sizzling, seductive smile. His eyes seemed to say, "How may I help you?" And his body language—the cool, confident, assured stance—offered a multitude of possibilities.

She continued to observe him, cautiously, and he continued to hold her gaze. Fire Captain Hightower didn't appear to know the meaning of the words *back down.*

Too bad.

Aisha shook her head with all the rejection she could

muster lacing her stare and posture. She even put on her best don't-even-try-it-or-think-about-it-brother glare and placed her hand on her hip, blocking his sensual assault with everything she could. It might have helped if she didn't find herself so incredibly attracted to him.

And what did the man have the nerve to do in the face of her rejection? He saw her shaking head and smiled as he nodded! He even mouthed the word *yes* before winking at her and leaving the room.

The air seemed to return to the room with a gush. The kids were being taught what to do. She gasped as she wondered who in hell was going to save *her?*

He couldn't just let her leave without asking her out. Could he? It wasn't every day that he met a woman who piqued his interest enough to even bother with the effort it took for any kind of approach. And she already had his adrenaline going at high speed.

She didn't seem particularly approachable or even open to his advances. That could be a problem. But he was never one to back away from a challenge. And something screamed in his head that she would be his biggest challenge yet. He just wanted to get to know her after all. What could be the harm in that?

"Excuse me, Ms. Miller." He caught up to her just as she and her teaching assistant led the students out of the building. "Can I speak with you for a moment? I promise not to take too much of your time. I know you have to get the little ones back to school."

He cleared his throat. He sounded like a sucker to his own ears. That wasn't good. He straightened his stance and put on a mental cloak of confidence. No matter how ill-fitting it felt at the moment, he needed something if he was going to get this sexy woman to give him the time of day and he was woefully out of practice.

She let out a breath and nodded at her assistant before walking over to him.

"Look, Captain Hightower—"

"Would you like to go out on a date sometime?" They had started talking at the same time, but only he continued and actually finished his sentence.

She stood there looking at him. She swallowed before opening her mouth and then she paused.

He took her pause as an opening for him to make his case. "Look, I don't do this kind of thing all the time, if that's what you're thinking. But I know for a fact that we'd both regret it if we don't go out on at least one date. So how about you give me your number and we square out the logistics later?"

Smooth.

Her head reared back and her hands found her hips. Again, he wondered how she made a straight-leg pair of navy blue slacks so sexy. His eyes followed each movement and remained fixed on her hips for a second too long. He shook his head and found her giving him the Aunt Esther "You-fish-eyed-fool" slanted-eye glare. She glanced at her students and then seemed to think better of telling off the fire captain.

"Thanks, but no thanks." She folded her arms

across her chest, her entire posture daring him to say another word.

"But…" He wanted to say they'd be good together. That he could feel it after only knowing her for a few minutes.

Was he coming on too strong?

Probably.

Did he have a choice?

Probably not, especially if watching the first woman who had managed to work her way past his shield and make him want more than a brief affair without even trying was any indication.

She rolled her eyes at him before plastering on an overly bright smile and turning to her students. "Say thank-you to Fire Captain Hightower for opening up the firehouse for our tour, boys and girls."

"Thank you, Fire Captain Hightower!" The boys and girls hollered. And with that they took off down the street and back to school.

He couldn't help but smile. He fully intended to take the cute and sassy kindergarten teacher out on a date.

"He shoots. He fumbles. He's outta here!" The rookie, Reggie Smith, had the nerve to be standing there grinning at Patrick as he chanted his little taunt. Then he added a little mock sympathy to boot. "Aww, better luck next time, Captain Hightower. Maybe if you got more practice, you'd have better game."

"Get back to work, rookie. I think the coffee is running low."

In addition to handling the student tours and anything

else the more seasoned firefighters didn't want to do, it was the rookie's job to make sure there was always fresh coffee. It was not the rookie's job to tease his superiors. But Patrick had other things to think about that were far more pressing. Things like: Why did she say no? And how could he get her to say yes? Those ranked high on his list....

"My, my, my, somebody has a big ol' fine sexy admirer. A big ol' fine sexy *Hightower* admirer! The single women at Mount Zion Baptist are going to mourn up a storm when the word hits that the last Hightower has bitten the dust." Toni started running off at the mouth as they led the children back into the classroom.

Aisha shook her head. She should have known her nosy little teaching assistant wasn't going to let the incident at the firehouse slide.

Toni was one of those long and lean sisters who wore style and fashion like it was her birthright. She had one of those chopped and blunt hairstyles that made her look like a rocker girl instead of a teaching assistant and part-time college student. She was in her late twenties and life was still an open book for her. And she apparently knew the fire captain, so getting her to give it a rest would be darn near impossible.

Impossible or not, Aisha knew she was going to try her best to ignore the girl.

"Nap time." She readied her little munchkins for their naps. When they awakened, it would be exercise time, math time, then time for them to go home.

Watching them resting on their cots with their little blankets and pillows made her heart full. All of a sudden she felt so glad that she had finally followed her heart and become a teacher. It had been a long and circuitous journey but she'd made it, and her life was on the right track. No way was she going to let some sexy fire captain turn her head.

"Have you thought about the book club? We're meeting this Saturday at my cousin Jenny's house. Everyone is bringing at least one other person. So I'm hoping you'll be my person. Be my person, ple-ase." Toni grinned and it was all Aisha could do not to laugh.

Aisha straightened one of the lopsided construction paper turkeys that her students had made by tracing their hands. It was only mid-October, but they started making holiday decorations earlier and earlier. Soon they'd be making paper Santas and stockings with their names on them. She then turned her attention back to Toni.

"You know I only like to read romance novels. If I join a book club, then I'm going to have to read sad and depressing books and Lord knows what else." She had seen enough sad and depressing in life and didn't need to read about it in her free time.

She had given the book club some thought, though. While she would love to make a few new friends in the area finally and have some adult company, as a single mom, she didn't have a lot of free time to read and what free time she did have she saved for her romance novels. A. C. Arthur, Ann Christopher, Brenda Jackson, Deatri King-Bey, Victoria Wells, Beverly Jenkins and LaConnie Taylor-Jones had first billing whenever she had a moment to spare.

"Plus, you know I don't like to leave Dillon with a babysitter, especially on the weekend. My ex finds every conceivable way to skip his visitations. And I'm not mad about that because I don't want my son around him anyway. But that means no weekends off for me."

"First of all, it would do us all some good to expand our horizons and read outside our comfort zones. I'm doing it because I want to read something besides all the boring stuff I'm reading in school." Toni shook her head and the razor-sharp asymmetrical cut moved with precision and then fell right back into place.

"And it will only be one book a month," Toni added. "You might like it. And for all those romance novels you're reading, you would think you would be more open to going out on a date with that fine Captain Patrick Hightower. Yummy… I can't believe you turned him down!"

"Oh, would you look at the time…" Aisha glanced down at her watch. "It's almost time to get these little ones up so they can get ready to go home for the day."

"Uh-uh, don't even try it. We've got five minutes. But I promise I'll leave it alone if you agree to go with me to the book club meeting. Just come to this first open meeting and see if you like it. Maybe we could even read a couple of those romance novels you like so much…"

"What about Dillon? It's too late for me to look for a sitter—"

"You don't need one. You can bring him along. My cousin Jenny has two kids of her own, a little boy and a little diva-in-training, and they'll more than likely be playing in another room. So you can *totally* bring Dillon with you. He'll have fun and you'll both make new friends."

"Well… I have wanted to meet new people. We've been in Paterson a few years, but I still haven't made a lot of friends outside of work. And Bill got all our Montclair friends with the divorce… I suppose I could go and check it out. But I'm telling you they need to read at least two romance novels."

"Great!" Toni bounced up and started putting away books and construction paper and anything else the children might have left out in the common areas.

Aisha smiled. At least she had gotten Toni to stop ragging her about Patrick. She had narrowly escaped that situation still on course. It would have been so easy to say yes to him. To give him her number and take a chance, even when he was everything she needed to avoid in a man.

The only place a larger-than-life alpha male like that could exist and not be a danger to those around him was in a romance novel. And the only way for her to change the cycle of abuse that plagued the women in her family was not to date and never be vulnerable again. As long as she kept her focus and stayed away from men like Patrick Hightower, she should be okay.

That should be a snap. She could *totally* do that. No problem.

Patrick who?

Patrick *freaking* Hightower, that's who! Of all the YMCAs in all the world, or at least in the north Jersey area, he had to walk into hers. Granted, she wouldn't have been there this evening if Dillon's usual karate class hadn't been rescheduled, forcing her to attend the Zuumba class instead of her normal Pilates. She tried to grab an exercise class while Dillon took his karate lessons and art classes at the Y. The family membership was in her budget, and the fact that she didn't have to spring for a sitter while she exercised and Dillon actually got to learn new things made the price more than worth it.

She had never seen Patrick Hightower at the Y before. It had been two days since she'd met him at the fire station, two days of her wondering what if she had said yes to his request for a date. It was bad enough he had invaded her mental space. Did he have to invade her gym, as well?

And here she was fresh out of class, sweaty, looking a mess with her hair pulled back in a ponytail, and she had to run into him. He looked great, perfect, with strong muscular thighs and arms in full view. God bless the person who'd turned those particular pieces of cotton into a T-shirt and shorts. He had a basketball in his hands and he looked as if he was about to shoot some hoops.

She was just about to pray that he wouldn't notice her when he looked right at her and walked—no, strutted—his fine self right over.

"Well, hello there, Ms. Miller. I didn't know you belonged to this Y. Why haven't I run into you here before?" Patrick offered that smile of his, that half-tilt, sparkly-eye thing he did apparently just to make her skin run hot.

"I'm not usually here during this time of day. My schedule got turned around." *And you can best believe it won't happen again now that I know I could possibly run into temptation on legs. Strong, long, take-me-now legs…*

"Listen, I think we may have gotten off on the wrong foot the other day and I—"

Another voice interjected, "Aisha, I'm so glad I didn't miss you. This schedule change has my day all screwed up. You said you would help me figure out these forms the next time the boys had karate. And I left them home and had to go back for them. Can you take a look at them now?"

Aisha turned and saw Mrs. Oliver walking over, waving a bunch of papers, and for a minute her brain had a disconnect. She shook her head to clear it and remembered that the widowed grandmother, who was raising her drug-addicted youngest daughter's children, had asked her for some help last week filling out the oldest child's financial aid forms.

When Mrs. Oliver reached them, her eyes sort of

squinted and her lips curved. "Oh, I can see you're busy. I can try and—"

"No, Mrs. Oliver, I'm not busy at all. We have a half hour before the boys are done with karate. Let's go over here and I'll try to help you as best I can. It's been a little while since I last had to fill out financial aid forms. They can be frustrating, but we'll get them done." Aisha turned to Patrick. "It was nice running into you again, Captain Hightower. Enjoy your game of basketball."

She then took off with her new savior, Mrs. Oliver, and found a quiet spot to help her with the forms.

Sure, she would now wonder what would have happened if Mrs. Oliver hadn't shown up. And seeing him in those shorts wouldn't do a thing to chip away his muscular image from her mind. But at this point running was the safest thing for her to do.

Patrick stared after Aisha and he couldn't help the smile that took over his mouth. It still felt foreign and he swore he'd never get used to grinning this much. But ever since he'd met her the other day, he'd found himself smiling more, especially when he thought of her. And he'd thought about her often during the past two days.

Even though it seemed as if she couldn't wait to get away from him, he sensed a spark there. And even though she was sweat-soaked from her workout, with her hair pulled back, she looked amazing. He glanced over to where she sat helping the older woman with the financial aid forms and he couldn't help but remember how she had calmly, patiently and lovingly consoled the little girl the other day. She clearly had a gift for helping others. He liked that. Her kind and generous spirit was refreshing and intriguing, and seeing her again worked only to make him all the more determined to get to know her better.

The rest of Patrick's rotation went by in a blur. He was pretty sure he knew what was happening to him. He had an inkling of a feeling as to why he couldn't get a prim, proper and prissy kindergarten teacher out of his head. But there was no way to know for sure. He had never felt these oddly fluttery...

What kind of man feels fluttery, anyway?

Just picturing her face made him want to burst out into a wide grin. He was laughing at the corniest jokes and in a damn good mood to boot.

He was hardly *ever* in a good mood. He typically avoided good moods like the plague. Good moods left people wide-open with their guard down, no defenses. Gruff suited him better. Gruff should have been his middle name. But something was going on with him that was making him, dare he even think it...happy. And fluttery.

Picking up his cell phone, he made three calls to the three men who would best be able to fill him in on the these weird feelings. His younger, married and in love brothers had all made the plunge into matrimony within the past three years.

Once he had two of the three of them at his house, he was beginning to think it wasn't a good idea after all. His brothers, Lawrence and Joel, both seemed as if they would rather have been anywhere but there. All the Hightower men took after their father in looks, and his father, James Hightower, was almost an exact body double for Richard Roundtree, the original Shaft. They were all tall, in shape and handsome, with mahogany complexions and killer smiles.

Patrick's younger brother, the second oldest after him, Lawrence, lounged in Patrick's favorite black leather recliner with his typical nonchalant stare. Lawrence was a narcotics detective with the Paterson Police Department and very little seemed to faze him.

Patrick had only seen Lawrence's cool, calm demeanor crack once. That was when Lawrence had met the woman who was now his wife. Lawrence had darn near turned himself into the woman's personal shadow and walked around like he couldn't figure out right from left for at least three months. And when he finally realized that it was love that had taken him out, he almost blew that.

Patrick frowned. Maybe it wasn't a good idea talking about any of this with his brothers after all. They probably wouldn't have useful advice, since they had each struggled in their situations. But they all had their women now and they were all happy....

"Are you going to sit there all night twisting up your face, grunting and mumbling to yourself, or are you going to fill us in on why we had to pull ourselves away from our very beautiful wives? I knew you'd turn into a grumpy old man one day, big bro, but the grumbling and mumbling is a bit much even for you." Joel, the family prankster, always had a joke or wisecrack ready to go.

There was always one jokester in every family. And, unfortunately for the Hightowers, their one had gone and found the other pea to his pod. Between Joel and his spitfire wife, Samantha, *no one* was safe. If one didn't have a joke or a wisecrack, the other one was more than willing to comply.

Joel sat on the black leather sofa, constantly checking his watch, with a wiseguy smirk on his face. He had finally gotten over his bad feelings about his career-ending injury and was content working at Hightower Security and no longer being a firefighter.

"I'm waiting for your baby brother to get here. I need all of you clowns here so I can do this once and only once." Patrick wondered what was keeping the youngest Hightower.

Even though Patrick had been the first to get married out of the bunch and the first and only one to get divorced, Jason Hightower had been the first to fall in love. He lost his heart to his wife, Penny, when he was barely ten years old. The childhood friends and teenage lovers had broken apart for fifteen years, but they were back together now, married and the parents of the cutest two-year-old girl and the most handsome seven-month-old little boy Patrick had ever seen, with the exception of Joel and Samantha's little ten-month old son.

Patrick was very biased when it came to his niece and nephews. He was becoming the world's largest Mr. Softie and those three blessings were the main reasons why. Being an uncle brought him a happiness he couldn't describe. It also brought a deep longing for a family of his own.

"You know Jason can never pull himself away from his family whenever he has time off. Little Cee Cee has him wrapped around her pudgy two-year-old finger. And he dotes on Jason Jr. so much, we're gonna have to take the little boy out every now and then when he gets older to toughen him up. Jason is almost as bad with his kids as Joel and Samantha are with Joel Jr." Lawrence shook his head in mock disgust.

"Like you're gonna be much better when Minerva has your baby. She's barely showing and you already can't stand to be away from her." Joel let out a hooting laugh.

"No, Joel. He could barely stay away from her from the first moment he set eyes on her. My brother the police officer officially became a stalker. I was worried about you, bro. I'm glad Minerva made an honest man out of you and gave you a legal reason to hang around her all the time." Patrick joined in Joel's laughter.

"Now both of y'all got jokes, huh? I'll tell you what. How about you get to whatever—" Lawrence's ringing cell phone stopped him midsentence.

"Hey, baby…" Lawrence's normally tough-guy tone went down a few octaves and Patrick immediately knew who was on the other end of the line. If the loving tone of voice didn't give it away, then the ear-to-ear grin certainly did. It had to be Minerva. And whatever she said had to be bad because his brother's grin fell into a deep frown and he cut Patrick a glaring look.

"That's cool, baby. You have fun with the girls. I'll see you when we both get home. I can just pick up something quick from the diner." Lawrence gave Patrick another angry scowl.

Food! How did Patrick know Lawrence's sour mood had something to do with food? Because Lawrence's mood could always change when it came down to him getting a good home-cooked meal.

Lawrence hung up his cell. "You owe me big-time, man. What do you have to eat in this dump? Apparently, Mom and Dad decided they wanted to spend some quality time with all their grandchildren and this freed Samantha and Penny to kidnap my wife and take her shopping for all the 'cute little maternity clothes she's going to need.'" Lawrence mimicked the high-pitched, gleeful sound his sisters-in-law made when they talked about clothes and shoe shopping. "So the wonderful home-cooked meal that my wife was going to make for me is no more and you have to feed me."

The doorbell rang and Patrick shook his head as he went to answer it. "Joel, order a pizza and some wings for your always hungry brother while I let baby bro in."

The pizza and wings came and they sat in the living room with a basketball game on the flat screen as white noise.

They didn't get a chance to hang out nearly as much as they used to before his younger brothers all got hitched. Patrick missed that sometimes, but what he got in return—with wonderful sister-in-laws, a niece, two nephews and a new baby on the way—more than made up for the male bonding time he was missing with his brothers. Still it was moments like these when they did hang out that made him happy to have them.

"So." Lawrence leaned back, rubbing his now full stomach, content for the moment, with a hint of a smile even. "What was so important that we all had to get over here tonight?"

"I think I know what it is." Jason shook his head. "Aw…man…did you find out that Courtney was moving back to Paterson?"

His ex-wife? Moving back to Paterson? *Say what?*

"What you talking 'bout, Jason?" Joel laughed at his own impression of Gary Coleman and everyone else just stared at him before turning back to Jason.

Patrick rubbed his chin as he waited for the anger and hurt to surface. It had been ten years since he had found Courtney in bed with another man. Patrick had come down with a severe case of the flu and he'd had to be relieved from his shift at the fire station. He had come home expecting his stay-at-home wife to pamper him and make him feel better.

Instead, flu or no flu, he had ended up opening up a can of whup-ass on the no good lawyer and church deacon he had found in bed with his wife. She begged forgiveness and wanted them to try counseling, but there was just no coming back from that as far as he was concerned. They had only been married for four years. He had hung up his player status at twenty-six to marry a woman he thought was true. And for many years he wondered if she had been cheating the entire time.

When the bad feelings didn't surface, he shrugged. "I hadn't heard she was moving back permanently and it really doesn't matter. It is ironic that she would pick now to move back, though."

"It wasn't like she had moved far away anyway. The chick was only in Trenton and she was in town often hanging out with her sorority sisters and having her monthly lunch with Aunt Sophie. She should have moved a whole lot farther away and she should have had the good taste to stay gone," Joel said.

Patrick sighed. He had figured out intricate ways to avoid running into his ex-wife through the years, stealth-spy ways. And he needed them because from the time the ink dried on the divorce papers, his Aunt Sophie had been trying to get him to take Courtney back.

He hadn't seen Courtney in at least six months, and that had only been in passing. Even his best avoidance skills were no match for two schemers on a mission. So he figured out a way to deal with seeing her and as the years went by, it bothered him less and less.

"Anyway, none of that is important. And it has nothing to do with why I asked to see you three knuckleheads. I need to pick your brains about the moment you knew that your wives were the one."

Jason tilted his head and put on his police detective inquisitive stare.

Joel's mouth dropped open and his eyes widened. He started laughing almost immediately.

Lawrence rubbed his chin and his signature know-it-all smirk graced his face.

Too late to turn back now…

"I mean, I know that Jason was pretty much a goner for Penny from the time he was a kid. Poor sap didn't stand a chance. And Joel, you walked around with that silly grin on your face all the time. We didn't think we would ever see you smile again after your accident and then one meeting with your physical therapist, Samantha, and you were *sprung*. And Lawrence, you took one look at Minerva and you turned into a stalker—"

"I wasn't a stalker!" Lawrence interrupted in a huff.

"Dude, you were damn close to it. I was worried I would have to arrest my own brother." Jason chuckled and Lawrence glared at him.

"Anyway, I wanted to find out from you guys—how did it feel? I realized that none of you had a clue you had just met the love of your life. You were too slow to see what the rest of us could tell just from looking at you. But—"

"Wait a damn minute! For somebody who obviously wants our help, you are being a little too free with the put-downs. I know that's how you are all the time. But if you want *my* help, you're going to have to be nicer." Joel folded his arms across his chest. "And for the record, I did not walk around with a silly grin on my face. And I realized that Samantha was the love of my life fairly quickly and put her on notice, as well. I was much quicker than the stalker cop over there."

"I was not stalking her! I was doing my job," Lawrence snapped.

"Anyway." Jason shook his head at Lawrence. "I'm with Joel. Big bro needs to be a little nicer if he wants our help. And he's going to have to come clean about why he wants our help. I don't know about y'all, but I need some more details."

"I need some more details, too," Joel said.

"Oh, I definitely need some more details," Lawrence offered gruffly.

Patrick eyed each of his brothers cautiously. He should have known these three jokers wouldn't have made this easy. He probably should have toned down his comments, since they had apparently gotten them all riled up.

He leaned forward. "I met a woman—"

"Oh, snap!" Joel stared at him with glee and mirth as he interrupted. "Samantha said that when the love bug bit your surly, grumpy behind it was going to take you down hard and fast. But this is ridiculous. You met her today and she's already got you calling for council from your younger, smarter, better-looking—"

"All right, can I finish? And tell my sister-in-law to stop talking about me. Anyway, I met a woman today, a kindergarten teacher who brought her class to visit the firehouse—"

"I used to love giving tours to the little kiddies. That was a fun part of the job. The kids really looked up to—" Joel cut him off again.

"Anyway…can I finish?" He glared at his brother.

"Oops. My bad. Go ahead, man." A sheepish expression crossed Joel's face.

"So, from the moment I set eyes on her when I welcomed the class to the firehouse, I felt weird. I wanted to keep looking at her. So I hung around for a little while as the rookie gave the tour and I even went out afterward and asked her on a date."

"Playa, playa…" Jason offered with a smirk. "So when are you taking her out? Is that what you need advice on, where to take her and how to impress her? It's been a minute since I've been in the game, but in my day, you know—"

"I'm not taking her out. *Yet.* She said she doesn't date."

"She doesn't date? What?" Perplexed, Lawrence frowned. "Wait… Was this a Catholic school? Did you hit on a nun? You know they don't always wear those habits and stuff anymore—" Lawrence started.

"It was a public school, and she wasn't a nun! And I'm not asking for advice on how to woo her once I get her to agree to a date." Disgusted at the thought that his younger brothers would even deign to think that they had more skills that he, Patrick grimaced. "I'm the reason you scrubs had any game to start with, and the last thing I need is advice about that from y'all. *Advice?* Please! When I taught y'all everything you know?"

"So what do you want?" Jason asked.

"I want to know if this urge to break out into a smile every time I picture her face, if the serious and steady thump in my chest every time I think about her, and this urge I have to find a way, any way, to see her short of *stalking…*" He shot Lawrence a glance. "I need to know if that's what it feels like when you meet her…*when you've met the one.* I think that's why I'm feeling this way and I don't want to be slow on the uptake like you three clow— I mean, you guys. So—"

"Yes. He's got it bad," Jason said with a chuckle.

"And it appears the last Hightower brother has been bitten by the love bug." Lawrence grinned.

"I don't know if she's *the one.* But it seems like you are recognizing her as the one. That's for sure. That's what it feels like. At least that's what it felt like to me," Joel offered.

"Me, too," Jason said.

"Yep. Me, too," Lawrence added.

"Didn't you feel like that with Courtney?" Joel asked.

Patrick thought about it for a full minute. He couldn't recall ever feeling like that from the first moment he had met his ex-wife. He remembered his aunt always pushing them together and he remembered slowly coming to enjoy her company and coming to love her. But he never felt anything like he felt now back then with Courtney.

"No. I didn't feel like this with Courtney."

Then, for the first time since his divorce, he started to think that maybe the failure of his marriage wasn't all Courtney's fault after all.

Chapter 3

"Did you finish your homework?" Aisha folded her arms across her chest and smiled at her son as he plopped down on the sofa and flipped on the television.

"I didn't have that much homework," Dillon offered after the short pause that had always been his tell sign.

Her ten-year-old son was a joy on most days. But morning cartoons made it difficult to get him dressed and out the door for school. And afternoon cartoons distracted him from his homework.

The copper-brown-complexioned child looked like a little male version of her, with the exception of the black curly hair he'd gotten from his dad. Her own hair reached the middle of her back and was chemically straightened. She seldom did more to it than curl the ends and pull it back with one of her many-colored and many-styled headbands. When she was feeling really adventurous, she pulled it back in a ponytail with a scrunchie. One day she would work up enough nerve to cut it all off into one of those funky hairstyles her teaching assistant, Toni, wore. But for now, she had a ten-year-old trying to get out of doing homework to deal with.

"You didn't answer the question, Dillon." She added extra inflection in her voice, walked over to the television and stood in front of it.

Sulking, Dillon turned it off and got up. "My favorite show will be off by the time I'm finished."

"Then maybe you should have started earlier and then you would have been done, huh? You were messing around back there doing everything but your homework. So get to it so that you can be done by dinner."

A spark of hope gleamed in his big brown eyes. "I could skip dinner and do my homework during dinner and watch my show now. Today we find out if the super ninja spider will—"

She had to cut him off. "Are you trying to say you'd rather watch those silly ninja spiders than eat one of my wonderful creations?"

Aisha knew she wasn't the greatest cook in the world—nowhere close. She experimented often with recipes that she saw being prepared on TV. But she also tried to make sure she put together simple healthy meals for her child and the little cartoon addict was going to eat his dinner.

"Well, Mom…" Dillon gave her one of his sly,

playful grins. "You could stand to watch a little less Food Network." He backed away as he spoke and his lanky body took off running when she picked up a pillow and tossed it at him.

"Just for that I'm *not* going to try the new recipe I found for a cool dessert."

"Yay! No test recipe this week!" her darling child yelled from his back bedroom.

"Oh, do your homework, you little prankster!" She laughed as she plopped down on the sofa and turned on the Food Network. One of these days she was going to get one of those recipes to turn out the way they did on TV.

Watching the cooking shows always soothed her mind and gave her something else to think about. She had never been a great cook and barely made the basics. It hadn't been a problem when she was married to William "Bill" Miller. He had always been fond of telling her he hadn't married her for her cooking or her brains.

The moment her verbally abusive former husband decided to up the ante and actually put his hands on her, her life took a detour. She only followed her desire to *really* learn to cook once she had gotten the courage to leave her husband, go back to school, finish her elementary education degree and got a job with the Paterson public school system.

Life was good now. She just had to make sure she resisted temptation and didn't let any man try to seduce her into giving up her new path. No matter how sexy and smoking hot he was…

Now that looks good. I bet I can totally make that.

She let her mind think of safer things as she watched
the Barefoot Contessa whip together the mocha buttercream frosting. How hard could that possibly be? It
looked easy enough. She grabbed the notepad she kept
by the sofa and started jotting down the ingredients and
directions. She might have missed some, but she was
sure she could wing it. She would try the dessert soon.
At least she could clear her mind of thoughts about the
sexy fireman.

Then, despite her best efforts, she suddenly envi-
sioned herself feeding the fireman delectable morsels
of her own mocha buttercream–frosted chocolate cake.
The vision looked too good to vanquish from her head
right away. So she let it linger. And then she had the
nerve to start daydreaming about mocha buttercream
frosting and that muscular frame of his. That's when she
knew she had to stop. Too bad she couldn't....

Chapter 4

Aisha sat in the Public School Number 21 faculty lunchroom, enjoying her turkey, avocado and tomato sandwich on whole wheat. During her hour-long break between her morning class being picked up and her afternoon class being dropped off, the building fire alarm went off. It wasn't a scheduled drill, so she hurried out of the building, helping other teachers control their students as she exited.

Standing outside in the brisk fall air, she only hoped that whatever fire team responded it wasn't one led by the sexy fire captain Patrick Hightower. The last thing she needed was a reminder of how she had totally blown off the finest man to ever make a move on her, *ever.*

She didn't regret turning him down. *Not really...*

But she certainly didn't need to see him again. His confident, bordering on cocky, approach let her know that he was probably a man just like her father, just like her ex-husband.

He was not a man she wanted or needed. She repeated those words like a holy mantra in her head and hoped that they would sink in.

When the fire truck and fire engine pulled up and she got a glimpse of *him* jumping off the truck like a dog-gone super action hero coming to save the day, looking fine in his full fire-repellant uniform, she cursed the mantra. Her mouth went dryer than the Sudan and she could have sworn her breath was starting to make soft little pants. He looked dead at her; at least she thought he zoomed right in on her before he went into the building.

The other firemen with him hardly seemed to matter. She barely registered their presence. It was something about the way his eyes seemed to take all of her in with one glance that left her blind, deaf and dumb.

She must have been imagining things. There was no way he had found her out of all the other teachers and the many students standing outside the building. She shook her head trying to clear the daze.

Not for me. Not for me. Not for me.

Maybe if she changed her mantra she'd stand a better chance. The image of Patrick's slow, seductive smile and simmering eyes came into her mind and she realized that all the mantras in the world wouldn't help her. She'd just have to be sure to stay away from him.

Since there was no smoke and the only heat she could sense was the sizzling sparks she felt whenever she thought of the fire captain, she figured that fate must have conspired with some little kid who was thinking it was a good idea to pull a prank by pulling the fire alarm.

She hoped the little rat was caught and suspended for an entire month—heck, the rest of the school year wouldn't be enough punishment for him bringing temptation in the form of the sexy fire captain into her world yet again.

Sure enough, there was no fire in the building. The school administrators were now looking for the child who had wasted the time of the fire department.

While they did that and the other teachers took their students back to class, Aisha watched the firemen get back in the truck. She told herself it was because she had to stand outside and wait for her afternoon kindergartners anyway. But deep inside she knew it was because she wanted to get just one more peek at Patrick.

Just because she couldn't have him didn't mean she couldn't look. Did it? What possible harm could be done by looking?

She regretted the thought as soon as she caught his dead-on stare once again. If she had any doubts about who he had been looking at the first time he zeroed in on her, they were all gone now. The rest of the teachers and students had gone back to their classrooms.

She watched as his sumptuous lips slowly curved, showing a hint of perfect white teeth and then the full bright grin hit her and sparked a powerful keening, needful emotion deep down in her gut.

What the heck was it? Lust? Desire? Wantonness? It had to be one of those. Whatever it was, she certainly wasn't giving in to it. No matter how much it was starting to ache just looking at him.

She let out a sigh when the truck started to pull off. Patrick kept looking at her, though. She could have sworn he kept looking at her until the truck reached the corner. And then he pointed from himself to her and she found herself smiling as she shook her head. He pointed between them again as he nodded and the truck turned the corner.

"Mmm-hmm. I see that, missy. You can't fool me. You want that fine Hightower man in a bad way, don't you?"

Rats! When had Toni crept up on her?

Her teaching assistant had had an emergency dental appointment because one of her fillings fell out, and had missed the morning class. Even though the little ones could be more than a handful, Aisha almost wished Toni had stayed out the entire day.

"Looks like I missed the fire drill and the fire, *too,* the way you two were heating things up out here. Dang, if he wasn't all the way up there in that truck fully clothed in that sexy fireman's uniform, I would have had to tell you two to go get a room."

"Stop playing. How's your tooth?"

"Uh-uh. Don't try to change the subject. What did I miss?"

"You missed a false fire alarm. I think it was one of those little roughneck-in-training eighth graders."

"Okay. Be like that, Aisha. But you wait until I have a sexy fireman giving me the ooo-baby-I-want-you-bad look. Don't think I'm going to give you the dish. Because I won't."

"Girl, you wouldn't be able to help yourself. You'd tell me everything as soon as the dude cracked the first smile at you."

Toni burst out laughing. "You know me so well!"

"Hello, Michaela. Stand in line as we wait for the rest of your classmates." Aisha shot Toni a quick glance to let her know the subject of Patrick Hightower was done as soon as the first parent walked up and dropped off her child.

"Oh, don't worry, missy, we're going to finish this conversation at book club tomorrow." Toni grinned. "Hey, Michaela! Are you ready for a fun afternoon?"

Michaela grinned back at Toni, showing a big, wide space in the front of her mouth where her two front teeth used to be. She nodded and giggled. That was a big change from the little girl who only a month ago had cried every time her mother dropped her off.

The rest of her twenty students came and soon she was in the classroom repeating everything she had taught the morning class earlier. But try as she might, she couldn't seem to get Patrick Hightower out of her mind.

He couldn't get out of his uniform and out of the station fast enough. Once his replacement was in, he headed out and rushed over to the school to try to catch Aisha before she left for the day.

They had gotten the alarm while they were waiting for their shift replacement and his gear was still up, so he had to take the ride. Luckily, it was just an alarm and not a fire.

Patrick showered quickly and put on his street clothes, all the while thinking about that sweet, hesitant smile that had crossed her delectable lips. If she really didn't want anything to do with him, then she needed to control her lips and never smile at him again.

Man! What was happening to him?

He didn't know. But he did know that he was ready to start thinking about a more long-term arrangement, certainly longer than his typical brief and hot encounters. He had a feeling it would take him longer to tire of the sexy schoolteacher—a whole lot longer.

If only he could get her to agree to a date with him…

He didn't know why she refused his request, but he had no intention of letting that stop him. So he planned to catch her as she left work today and ask her again. He was going to keep asking her until he got a yes.

He parked his SUV and hopped out in front of the school just in time to see her walking to her car. Running up beside her, he caught her. She shrieked, jumped and stumbled, dropping her bag on the ground.

Shock waves covered his skin and his mouth suddenly felt like it was full of cotton candy. It wasn't just dry, it was sticky and he seemed to have forgotten how to move it to get words out.

"You scared me! You can't just come running up to people like that. What is *wrong* with you?" With one hand patting her chest and the other on her hip, she looked the picture of beauty.

She spoke with perfect inflection and a healthy dose of righteous indignation, even as she struggled to catch her breath.

He, on the other hand, couldn't say a word. So he bent down to pick up her bag. When he handed it to her, his fingers grazed hers.

Tingles. And something else…

"Sorry I scared you." His mind finally managed to figure out how the mouth, tongue, lips thing actually formed words. "I just wanted to catch you before you got away. I really think you ought to let me take you out on a date."

The eyebrow over her left eye rose slightly and her chest puffed up. He wished she hadn't taken that huff of air because now his eyes fixated on her perfect, perky breasts and that probably wasn't going to make her amenable to his request.

He forced his glance away just in time to catch her glaring stare and clenched teeth.

"I just don't understand why a beautiful woman like you has taken herself off the dating market. I don't see a ring on your finger. Are you married?"

"It's none of your business why I don't date."

"I sense a serious connection between the two of us and I know I'm not the only one." This was not happening to him. It couldn't be. She was rejecting him *again?*

He had to make her see what he saw. There was no way she didn't feel what he felt.

"I know you felt it when I touched you just now. The jolt that felt like your heart was about to jump all the way up into your throat? The rapid beating of your heart that makes you feel like you had one too many cups of espresso followed by a Mountain Dew."

"I learned to control my hormones in high school, Captain Hightower. You'd do well to do the same."

"It's not just hormones. If it were just that, I wouldn't be out here trying to convince you to go out on one date with me."

"Well, I'm sorry you've wasted your time. I'm not going out with you. And I'd thank you not to show up at my place of employment again with your requests. It's not going to happen."

He paused and studied her. If he hadn't been attuned to her every breath, every shudder and pull, he might have missed her trying to firm her resolve, as if she were trying to convince herself.

Then, he might have decided she was right. After all, he had never had to beg for a date or work this hard to get a woman's attention before. He was a Hightower. He had a line of women waiting for the day he was ready to open his heart for more than a brief fling, and those were just the single women at his family church of Mount Zion. He was a catch, and begging was not his M.O.

He took a step back and smiled. He wasn't a glutton for punishment or on some sadomasochistic trip. He should just walk away from this pursuit now…

But he did feel more alive in the few days he'd been trying to get the beautiful schoolteacher to say yes to a date than he had felt in a long time. He couldn't walk away.

"So I guess I'll take that as a no?"

Prim and proper in her pose and body language, she opened her mouth and closed it before she simply nodded her head. Her pretty reddish-brown face showed the slightest hint of hesitation as she sucked in her bottom lip and nibbled on it.

He couldn't help it. He reached out and touched her cheek and there it was. That jolt. That spark. Her eyes widened and he knew without a doubt that she felt it, too.

"Are you married, Aisha? You got a man? Is that it? Is that why you won't let me take you out on a date?"

She looked up at him, her eyes deep pools of rich brown sugar. "I'm divorced and I'm really not looking for another relationship. It's not high on my priority list. It really has— Well, it really has nothing to do with you."

"Did he hurt you?" He had to know what her ex-husband did to make her take her lovely self out of the game.

There was no way he was going to let any of their past relationships threaten the wonderful feeling of what-could-be that bubbled between them.

She stepped back and his hand fell away from her face. Even though he could tell that she didn't want to, she reached up and touched the space where his hand had rested before she took a big gulp of air, swallowed and then pursed her lips.

"That's none of your business. And this conversation, *you touching me* every chance you get, all of it is highly inappropriate and I'd thank you to *cut it out!*"

Her brown-sugar gaze crystallized into sharp points and he had to chuckle. She was the sweetest-looking woman he'd ever seen, even when she was angry, *especially* when she was angry. As if brown-sugar daggers could really do him any harm. Her glare didn't scare him at all. It made him want her even more.

"I'll let you go for now. But I want you to know that we are going to have our date sometime in the near future." He ran his hand across her cheek again just so he could feel the jolt. "I'll see you around, Aisha. You can count on that."

He turned and walked away then, because he wasn't exactly sure that he wouldn't pull her into his arms and kiss her senseless if he stood there looking at her a moment longer.

Sophie Hightower glanced at her watch and frowned. Courtney was late. Why she still bothered with the girl was beyond her. She had all but made sure her favorite nephew met and fell in love with Courtney years ago, and the silly girl had cheated and broken Patrick's heart.

Sophie glanced around the small eatery. Courtney had picked this little sandwich shop. Sophie brushed a crumb off the ecru tablecloth. Courtney certainly wouldn't be allowed to pick again. With crumbs on the table and the dingy tablecloths, how could she trust that the silverware would be clean?

If Sophie didn't know that Courtney was a good girl from a strong, upstanding family, she would have given up on the girl a long time ago. Even though she had cheated on Patrick, Courtney was still a million times better than those unworthy women her other nephews ended up marrying. And if Sophie could find a way to get Courtney and Patrick back together, at least she would have an ally in the family. And she needed an ally badly.

"Hi, Sophie. Sorry I'm late." Courtney swept into the restaurant, gave Sophie a peck on the cheek and sat down opposite her at the small table.

"It's okay, Courtney. I was just busying myself thinking about what we can do to get you back in the good graces of my nephew."

Courtney laughed. "If you can think of something I hadn't thought of and tried when he first filed for divorce, then by all means do so. I tried every trick in the book to make him forgive me for my mistake, and he wouldn't budge. I hope that time and space has mellowed his stubborn streak and his anger. Because I want my husband back."

Sophie studied the young woman. She had certainly matured over the years. Truth be told, neither Courtney nor Patrick had been ready for marriage. They were both young and still way too selfish at the time. Sophie could see that, and if she hadn't been worried about what kind of woefully inappropriate woman Patrick might end up with if she listened to his mother, Celia Hightower, the constant thorn in Sophie's side, then Sophie would have told them to wait awhile.

"You do seem like you're a little bit more ready to be a wife now. And I have to say I would love it if you and Patrick got back together. Once Patrick has a wife and a family, my brother will pass the house down to his oldest living son. And it would be nice to have a woman worthy of bearing the Hightower name in that house again. Do you know that Celia has had my brother James ban me from the house?"

"Again? What happened this time? What's her problem? Lord knows she never liked me and I never liked her, either. She never really got in our business or anything like that," Courtney paused and glanced at Sophie with a smirk. "But I just know she didn't try to get Patrick to take me back."

Sophie wondered what that little smirk was about. Courtney needed to be glad Sophie had been in their business. If she hadn't been, Courtney would not have married Patrick in the first place. Some people needed to have a little more gratitude. But she couldn't be concerned with that now. There was no time.

"At least it would have been time well spent getting you and Patrick back together. You should have seen how hard Celia worked to get Jason back together with that video vixen daughter of a crackhead, Penny Keys. Now we have all kinds of recovering addicts and former jailbirds at the family gatherings! And that's not the latest. My nephew Lawrence married a little gangster girl from South-Central California of all places. I call her little orphan anger because she doesn't have any living family at all. Have you ever heard of such a thing?"

Courtney burst out laughing. "I can't believe you called the woman Little Orphan Annie."

"I didn't. I call her little orphan *anger.* The girl has a smart mouth on her and she was extremely rude to me when I tried to give her advice that Lawrence might not be the man for her. But all that is beside the point. The point is that Patrick is my last chance. Celia has built her a little army and they have all but fazed me out. If you can atone and make Patrick take you back, when you two are in the house, it won't matter what Celia does."

"I don't know if your plan will work. Patrick has done a pretty good job of avoiding me through the years. At first it was cool, because I needed time to lick my wounds after messing up so badly. But after a while… I'm just not sure he'll ever forgive me. But I want him back. And when Patrick and I have kids, I want you in that house with us helping me, Sophie."

Sophie mentally rolled her eyes. The girl was such a suck-up, but she needed her if she was going to make this work. So Sophie would give as good as she got. "I'll certainly be there. This is going to work. What's your plan?"

"I don't have a plan." Courtney frowned. "You always tell me what to do."

"Well, I didn't tell you to cheat on your husband, did I? You came up with that little plan all on your own." This time she rolled her eyes for real. You just couldn't get good help these days.

Sighing, Sophie leaned forward to school her co-conspirator. "You need a way for him to see you. You know, he still keeps his spare key in the same place…"

Chapter 5

The book club was actually starting to seem like a pretty good idea. Of course, Toni, for all her "Be my person" requests, was running late and had left her alone. But Dillon seemed to hit it right off with Toni's cousin's daughter and son. And Aisha was more than ready to meet some new people. The other three women seemed really nice.

"So why don't we get started by introducing ourselves and saying a little bit about what kinds of books we like to read?" Jenny, Toni's cousin and their hostess, took a seat on the plush cream sofa and the three of them turned their attention to her. The short and pleasingly plump cinnamon-complexioned woman had a bubbly demeanor and Aisha could see her being an excellent receptionist. Her entire aura was welcoming.

"My name is Jennifer Saunders. But everyone calls me Jenny or Jen. I'm a receptionist at a physical therapy clinic and the married mother of two. I have a ten-year-old girl and a seven-year-old son. I love to read mystery novels mostly. I just love a good whodunit. Some of my favorite authors are Barbara Neely and Valerie Wilson Wesley." She turned to the woman on her right, signaling that it was her turn to go.

The young woman appeared to be in her mid- to late twenties and reminded Aisha of that hot new Hollywood actress, Lauren London. Her long, naturally curly hair was pulled away from her pretty face with one of those stylish blinged-out hairpins. She had a hip, youthful energy about her that reminded Aisha of the now-seriously-late Toni.

"My name is Minerva Hightower and my sister-in-law, Samantha—" she pointed to the beautiful dark-chocolate sister sitting next to her before continuing "—invited me to join you guys in the book club because she knew I would read anything between two covers with a spine. I'm sort of a bookaholic. I'm also a newly-wed. I've been married a little over a year. I'm finishing up my MSW and just found out that I'm almost four months' pregnant."

When the young woman spoke, there was something about her accent that let Aisha know she wasn't from Jersey. Everyone rushed to congratulate Minerva immediately, including Aisha, but in the back of her head, she couldn't help but wonder if the two Hightower women were somehow related to Patrick.

They said they were sisters-in-law. One could be his sister and the other could be his wife for all she knew. How awkward would that be?

Samantha introduced herself and apparently she was a doctor of physical therapy.

Soon it was Aisha's turn to introduce herself. Not one woman in the group had mentioned romance novels in the lists of books they like to read. She was suddenly feeling out of place and wondering where the heck Toni was. What would these other, seemingly happily married women with interesting jobs and eclectic reading tastes think of a divorced single-mom kindergarten teacher who steals away snatches of time to devour African-American romance novels?

She needed to go into the back room, grab her son and break the hell out of there before she had a chance to find out what they thought.

Wait a second, she thought, halting all her negative ramblings. She was just as good and just as smart as anyone else. She certainly wasn't ashamed of finally having the courage to break the cycle of violence in her family by divorcing her abusive husband. And she had worked darn hard raising a small boy alone and going back to school to become a kindergarten teacher.

Building back her self-esteem after years of a verbally abusive marriage had been hard, and it was clearly something she would have to continue to work on. She gave herself a mental shake to shore up her courage and introduced herself. Before she knew it, she was spilling out her introduction and waiting for the first person to even look like she had something sarcastic to say.

What she found instead surprised her.

"Girl, I love romance novels, too, especially the African-American ones. I'm addicted to them and my soaps, girl! I just *love* some *love*. I just didn't know what you all would think about my reading choices." Jenny gave an embarrassed chuckle. "So I left them out."

"Shoot, I cut my teeth on Arabesque when I was a preteen. My mom was sick, dying of AIDS, and she used to have me read her novels to her because she knew I liked to read," Minerva added.

"And these two got me hooked on them now. They keep me nice and romantically ready for my handsome husband." Samantha grinned widely when she mentioned her husband.

Aisha wondered if the man that put that smile on Samantha's face was Patrick Hightower.

They bonded and connected for over half an hour about their love for romance novels. They all had their top ten and all of their top ten favorites included the two BJs, Brenda Jackson and Beverly Jenkins.

"Well, since we all like African-American romance novels, I think we know what genre our first book will be," Jenny folded her hands on her lap and smiled.

"Romance!" all four women said in unison.

After setting up the parameters of the book club and deciding on a first book, a few of the women sat in Jenny's den chatting and continuing to get to know one another. Toni finally showed up and Aisha thought about reading her the riot act, but she'd had too much fun with the other women and had a good vibe about the possibilities for some new friendships, so she decided she would let Toni slide this one time.

"So tell me how's everything with you and that fine Hightower husband of yours. I bet he's loving being a new dad." Jenny playfully shoved Samantha's shoulder. "One day I'm going to have to tell you all how Samantha pretty much owes being married to the hottest man next to my Walt to my persistence in getting her to give the fine Joel Hightower a chance."

Aisha felt a gush of breath whoosh out of her mouth and it startled her. Why should she feel anything like relief just because Samantha wasn't married to Patrick?

"I would have come around eventually. I didn't need your nagging. Plus, Joel was a man on a mission. And nothing can stop a Hightower man once he has his sights on the woman he wants," Samantha said with a giggle.

"I know. Lawrence even arrested me a couple of times. Talk about a Hightower man getting his woman!" Minerva broke out laughing. "He's a real overachiever, my Lawrence."

Aisha broke out into a wide grin. Neither woman was married to Patrick.

Okay, missy, why do you care?

"Speaking of Hightowers…" Toni glanced at her and Aisha gave the woman the closest thing she could to a glare without calling too much attention to them.

"The last Hightower standing, that fine fire captain, Patrick Hightower, has the hots for our Aisha here." Toni burst out into a giggle and moved away from Aisha as quickly as she could.

"Toni, stop making stuff up. We read fiction in the book club—we don't create it." Aisha let out a nervous chuckle.

"I'm a witness. I saw it with my own eyes. I saw the great Patrick Hightower go down. The man couldn't keep his eyes off her. And he seemed genuinely upset that she wouldn't budge." Toni added fuel to the fire, refusing to let the conversation die.

Aisha cut her eyes at Toni. "Sure he was upset— because he's probably not used to hearing the word *no* when he asks for a date."

"Well, now, that is probably true. I don't recall very many women that would tell a Hightower man no when he asked for a date, unless you count my friend Samantha here. She played hard to get for…oh…about a minute with Joel." Jenny laughed and slapped her knee. "I thought they weren't going to ever get together. They had me addicted to their little drama like I am to my soaps."

"Anyway…" Samantha rolled her eyes at Jenny. "This isn't about me and Joel. It's about Aisha and Patrick."

"There is no Aisha and Patrick," Aisha offered with a smile.

Minerva slanted her eyes and pursed her lips. "Well, after everything that happened with his ex-wife, that man deserves some happiness."

"What happened with his ex-wife?" The question fell out of Aisha's mouth before she could stop it.

Why did you ask that? You don't care. Get your son and get out of here.

"Oh, I went to high school with both of them, so I can tell you that story from the beginning. Someone else would have to pick up the later end, though. I only have gossip and hearsay about the later years. But I will say that Courtney Phillips grew up in a very strict household. Her parents barely let her go outside all through grammar school and high school and they kept her hemmed up in the church." Jenny twisted up her lips and twirled her neck before continuing. "But anyone with an eye could see the girl was a slut waiting to happen and looking for a place to be all the slut she could be. She had a lot of people fooled by her goody-goody demeanor, especially Patrick. What a waste. A lot of girls in our high school would have married him. And we were all shocked and appalled when we found out about eight years after high school that he had married Courtney. I just guessed the only way she could get from under her family's thumb and finally be free to turn into the wild thang she was destined to be was to marry someone."

"All I know is he came home early from work one day, sick as a dog, and found his wife in bed with another man." Samantha added what Jenny left out.

"Oh, my God! That's awful!" Aisha knew a lot about cheating spouses and she wouldn't wish that kind of pain on anyone, especially the sexy fire captain.

"Yeah, awful for that young church deacon Patrick

caught her with. Joel said that they were lucky the man was too ashamed to press assault charges, because Patrick put a hurting on the man and kicked Courtney out."

"Hmm… So Patrick is violent? I teach my kindergartners to use their words for a reason. I don't condone hitting or violence." She couldn't help the self-righteous know-it-all tone she used, because she finally felt vindicated in turning Patrick down. She couldn't be with a violent man. She should have known a man like that would have a violent streak. Good thing she'd said no to him.

"Patrick doesn't condone hitting, either. And from what I can tell he isn't the violent type. Anyone who has seen him with his niece and nephews can see that he's really a gentle, loving teddy bear." Samantha smiled and then frowned. "He is grumpy, though. And he was bitter for years. And a bit gruff… And he probably broke a lot of hearts over the years because he wasn't ready to trust." She broke out into a grin again.

Aisha swallowed as she pictured Patrick's sultry gaze and remembered what it did to her pulse.

Who was she kidding? She didn't stand a chance.

"Well, enough of this gossiping about Captain Hightower. It's time for my son and I to go on our weekly date at Friendly's, where we both love the Reese's Peanut Butter Cup sundae. In fact, that's where we're going for dinner now. And after that I'm going to stop by the bookstore to pick up our book club pick and the latest Brenda Jackson, and then I'm going home to curl up with a book."

"See, she's crazy, y'all. Curling up with a book when she got that big, strong, strapping man sniffing after her. Somebody tell me where is the rhyme and reason in that!" Toni fell back on the sofa in mock disgust and placed her hand over her forehead.

Aisha laughed at her bigmouth, overly dramatic friend. "On that note…I'm out of here. Dillon and I have sundaes at Friendly's with our names on them. I'll catch you ladies next month. I'm really excited about the book club. Ms. Toni, I'll see you Monday."

As Patrick parked his SUV in the Friendly's parking lot and got out of the vehicle, he was a man on a mission. It was only when he entered the restaurant and saw Aisha sitting there with the most adorable little boy who looked just like a little male version of her with thick jet-black curls on the top of his head that Patrick started to question the wisdom of just showing up at the place.

When he'd gotten off the phone with his sisters-in-law—one actually on the phone and the other yelling excitedly in the background, both saying, "We met your schoolteacher"—he knew two things. One, he was going to pop Lawrence and Joel upside their heads when he saw them again for telling his business. And two, he had to try one more time to get Aisha to go on a date with him.

The shocked expression on Aisha's face when he walked up to their table was followed by a brief pout and then a phony, syrupy-sweet smile. She was wearing another one of those sweater sets, a pink one, and some gray slacks with her signature pearls.

He thanked the heavens that she apparently had something against making a scene in front of children. First, her kindergartners had saved him from being told off by her and now her son.

"Hi, Aisha. It's good to see you again."

She pursed her lips and swallowed, squinting her eyes just enough to let him know she wasn't buying anything he was selling.

"Hello, Captain Hightower. Fancy meeting you here at Friendly's of all places. Dillon, say hello to Captain Hightower. He's a fire captain with the Paterson Fire Department. Remember, I told you that I took my class to tour the fire station and learn about fire safety."

The young boy looked up at him with wide, appreciative eyes and tons of awe. "You're a real fireman? A *for real* fireman? Wow! I've never seen a real one up close. My teacher hasn't taken us to the station and Mom wouldn't let me miss school so that I can go with her class."

The young boy's excitement was contagious and Patrick felt the special energy that suffused him whenever he was around his niece and nephews take over. The need to be cool, lovable Uncle Patrick was hard to resist on a good day, and it was even harder now that he was also trying to put his best foot forward with Aisha.

"Oh, well, we'll have to remedy that. I'll just have to have you and your mom in for a personal tour just for you. Would you like that?"

"Awesome! Yes! I'd love that." The young boy started grinning from ear to ear.

"Of course, it would have to be okay with your mom, too. Is that all right with you, Aisha?"

"Please, Mom. Please!"

"Sweetie, we can't bother the firemen with personal tours and stuff. They have jobs to do. And I'm sure Captain Hightower has better things to do than give us tours. And it would have to be on a weekend because—"

"The weekend is fine. In fact, I'm off today and to-morrow. I could pick you both up Sunday afternoon after church and give you a tour, and then maybe treat you both to dinner afterwards. We could even come back here if this is your favorite place. I have to say they make the best Reese's Peanut Butter Cup sundaes I've ever tasted."

"Yes! No test recipes two days in a row! Please say yes, Mom. Please."

Aisha shot her son a look and then she slanted her eye at Patrick. "That's enough joking about my cooking, young man. And you…" She tightened her jaw and he could tell she was counting to ten before she plastered on a smile. "I'll certainly be having a talk with you soon. But for now, we would be happy for the tour tomorrow. We can meet you at the station at around two. But we probably won't be going to dinner with you afterward."

"Aw, man! So close! Captain Hightower, would you like to have dinner with us now? I want to hear about how you fight the fires. That's so cool. I think I want to be a fireman when I grow up—either that or a cop or an astronaut."

Aisha opened her mouth and closed it before finally nodding at him in approval and swallowing as if she had just gulped down a bitter pill. "You can certainly join us if you don't have other plans, Captain Hightower. Dillon is going through a stage where he is fascinated with firemen and policemen."

"Well, then I'd really better sit down because two of my brothers are police detectives, so I know a little something about policemen, too. In fact, most of the men in my family are either cops or firemen." Patrick smiled when he saw the way Dillon's eyes lit up at that tidbit of information.

"Thank you, Aisha. I'd love to share a meal with you and your son. He seems like an amazing kid and I'd really like to get to know the two of you better, if that's okay." He tentatively slid into the booth next to the person he hoped would be his new ally. Little Dillon seemed thrilled and launched right into a discussion about fires, police chases, sports and all kinds of stuff.

By the time they had finished their meals, Patrick has already offered to help the young man with his pitching, because his mom "threw like a girl." Aisha had even loosened up about midway through the meal. She even laughed a little. By the time he walked them out to their car and they got Dillon inside, Patrick was feeling as if he had made a ton of progress with Aisha. At least until she closed the door and didn't get inside her car and instead turned to him with the iciest glare he had ever seen. Good thing Dillon was in the car. Patrick was sure that seeing such an expression on his mom's face would have scared him.

"Look here, mister." She calmly stated between clenched teeth. "I don't know what kind of game you're playing. But I told you I *don't* date." She was losing a little bit of that air of prissiness and had become a little gritty. He liked that, too.

"And I don't appreciate people trying to pit my son against me." She poked him in the chest and he felt a bolt of sensation. She must have felt it, too, because she quickly pulled her hand away before continuing.

"So you need to cut it out now. I can't believe you just showed up and bulldogged your way into my evening out with my child. I am very particular about the people I have around my son, Patrick. And I can't have him getting attached to another man who won't be around."

"But I want to be around. I want to—" He felt the need to reassure her, but she cut him off.

"You *won't* be around because I *don't* date. We are *not* starting something here. And the sooner you realize that the better."

He shook his head. "Love, it's already started whether you know it or even acknowledge it."

Her brows furrowed and her bottom lip stuck out in the cutest little pout. He couldn't help himself; he quickly and lightly brushed his lips across hers. And even though she didn't slap him, he regretted it when he was done. That light brush sent a jolt of electricity pulsing through his veins and it was not nearly enough. He wanted to take her into his arms and kiss her soundly, thoroughly and deeply. He wanted to kiss away any hostility and doubt she might have had. He wanted to kiss her as if her ten-year-old son weren't in the car waiting for her.

He cleared his throat and backed away for a minute. He couldn't kiss her like that—not yet anyway.

"Good night, love. I'll see you and Dillon tomorrow. I just ask that you think about giving me a chance, giving us a chance. See you later."

He walked away then. Because he knew that he wouldn't be able to stop himself from kissing her for real if he stayed there any longer.

Chapter 6

The expression on her son's face as they left the fire station placed a lightness in her heart that she hadn't felt in years. Dillon grinned the way he did when he was able to finish his homework in time to catch those super ninja spider cartoons he loved.

She would probably keep the picture she'd snapped of him with Patrick's fireman's hat dwarfing his head on her phone until the end of time. She was almost tempted to look at it again and they had only taken it less than thirty minutes before.

The magic of the moment seemed to be at a standstill as the three of them now stood outside the fire station. Would she be the one to kill the moment? Or would she let it flow and let Patrick take them to dinner as he wanted to?

It wasn't *technically* a date since she had her son with her. And she was kind of hungry…

She glanced at Patrick, who was standing there trying his hardest not to push or come on too strong. He was holding back and that made him all the more endearing.

"I don't know, guys…" She still didn't trust the idea of spending even more time with Patrick.

He was too handsome. He was too intense. He was too good with her son. He was too damn perfect to be real and she was not falling for that crap again.

Been there, done that. Got the scars and crummy divorce settlement to prove it!

"Come on, Mom. I promise I'll do my homework as soon as I get home all week before I turn on the TV and—"

She slanted her eye at her little lying child.

Dillon giggled as he shifted from one foot to the other and bounced up and down, adding the anxious factor to his already pleading posture. "I'll try really hard, Mom. I promise."

She glanced at Patrick, who still hadn't said anything. She inhaled and let out her breath slowly. At least he wasn't trying to use Dillon to double-team her the way he had the night before. Maybe her little talk with him before she had gotten in the car had worked after all.

"Okay. But we should let Captain Hightower pick the place. I'm sure he'd rather eat someplace besides Friendly's."

"Actually, Friendly's is fine. It's the company I'm

interested in. I'd have dinner anywhere as long as you and your amazing son were there. And remember, no 'Captain Hightower'—Patrick is fine. Oh, and why don't we take my car? I can drop you off back at your car when we're done."

It did sort of make sense to take one car. Just as it was starting to make sense to stop fighting her attraction to Patrick and just see where things went between them.

What kind of crazy thought was that?

Just one afternoon with the man and she was already breaking down! She'd have to do a better job at keeping her barriers up. Patrick Hightower was proving to be a force to be reckoned with.

Riding in his luxury SUV felt too nice. The soft butter leather seats that apparently heated up to keep a person's bottom nice and toasty also had the nerve to feel like sitting on a cloud.

"So what's your deal, Patrick? What do you want? Because I told you—"

"I know. You don't date." He cut her off with a chuckle.

The deep barreling sound made her stomach dip and shift. It must have been the heat from her seat that had her feeling flush. The rich sound flowing from his lungs would have been infectious if she weren't annoyed at her body's other reactions to the sound. Things like her nipples tightening and her throat becoming the Sahara had no business happening.

She twisted her lips to the side and swallowed, then swallowed again and again.

"Listen, I would just like the chance to get to know you and Dillon a little better. It's not a date. And as soon as you start to feel uncomfortable, we can stop. It's just dinner. And from what Dillon was telling me about your concoctions when you went to the ladies' room a little while ago, it would be cruel and unusual punishment to wave Friendly's in front of the kid and take it away now."

Both Patrick and Dillon burst out laughing then, and she turned to glower at her treacherous kid. Dillon shrugged his shoulders and grinned.

"Mom can make some stuff really good," Dillon offered with a giggle. "It's the new recipes that she finds and tries to make that always end up yucky."

"Okay, little traitor, it's chicken and rice and peas for you from now on. Here I was trying to expand our horizons and give us more sophisticated palates." She folded her hands across her chest.

Patrick continued laughing as he started the car. "If you want to, you can try out some of your concoctions on me." He turned to her and she caught the sweetest, most sincere expression she had ever seen on a man.

Yes, she would certainly need to work on shoring up her defenses with this guy. They were probably already seriously breeched.

"I'd be happy to help you with your pitching, Dillon. We could go out to the park and practice on my days off, as long as you keep to that promise you made your mom about finishing your homework." Patrick turned to Aisha to see if it was okay with her.

She nodded slowly, but didn't say a word. In fact, she had been very quiet the entire meal. No words, no comments, no nothing.

They were sitting in the same booth at Friendly's as they had the night before, the booth that he had started to think of as *their* booth after only two outings. They had finished their food and were waiting for dessert.

He was starting to think that he shouldn't have inched his way into her world like this. But what was he supposed to do? She wasn't going to give him a chance. And something deep in his soul demanded that he have a chance, that he pursue this woman in a way he had never pursued another.

"And if it's okay with your mom, I'd love for you to consider joining the Little League team my brothers and I coach when the season starts up."

"Oh, Mom, can I?" Dillon could barely get the words out for all his bouncing excitement.

Patrick really liked Dillon and he'd been honest when he told Aisha that he wanted to get to know her and her son. The boy was extremely well-mannered and adorable. And at the moment, Dillon was the one who seemed the most open to actually giving Patrick a chance. As much as Aisha clearly loved her son, Patrick knew that having Dillon's stamp of approval couldn't hurt.

"What's your favorite sport, Dillon?"

"I like them all—baseball, football, basketball and soccer. But my favorite is basketball."

"Have you ever been to see a game?"

"No, my dad… No, I haven't." Dillon's normally happy face took on a sour expression.

Aisha closed her eyes for a moment and then opened them. "My ex-husband has been promising to take Dillon to a Nets game, but when things get busy at the law firm, he has to cancel. I keep telling Dillon, I'll save up and get us some tickets, but Dillon doesn't want to go with a *gi-rl*." She reached out and mussed the curls on the top of Dillon's head.

Brightening up a little at his mom's loving touch, Dillon inched away, laughing. "M-o-m… You wouldn't like it or be able to explain stuff to me or anything."

Seeing an opening and having no shame about taking it, Patrick jumped in. "How about I take us all to see a game? That way, I can help explain stuff to you and your mom. Maybe we can boost her sports knowledge a little so that after a while she won't seem so girly."

"Cool!" Dillon shouted with glee.

"Hey, I like being girly! There's nothing wrong with being girly."

Patrick grinned at her. She certainly had that right. There was nothing wrong with her girly attributes, nothing at all. He cleared his throat. Something told him that if he dared to voice those thoughts it would ruin the light mood that was developing.

"I can probably get us tickets to the Giants next weekend. Would you like to see a football game?"

"Yeah! All right!" Dillon pumped his little fist in the air.

Aisha pursed her lips and squinted before shaking her

head and slowly smiling. "You're not playing fair, Patrick."

"All's fair, love, all's fair." He held up his hands in mock innocence as he stared at her long enough for her to grasp his meaning.

At that moment he realized that he would give her as much time as she needed to get with the program, but he wasn't going to give up and he wasn't about to let her push him away.

Once he drove them back to her car, Aisha had to admit to herself that she was almost sad to see their day ending. The entire day, from Dillon's glee at the fire station to the mock speed sundae-eating contest the three of them had during dessert, had her thinking that that must be what a real family felt like. She couldn't remember ever laughing and having that much fun as a family when she was with her ex-husband. She had certainly never felt it growing up with her mom and dad.

And yet, here she was with Patrick Hightower, laughing and giggling like a schoolgirl who didn't know just how bad it hurt to fall in love and have that love stomped on and thrown back in her face.

"I'm going to follow you guys and make sure you make it home safely," he offered.

He had been so generous with his time and money that evening, she really couldn't envision taking more. "That's okay, Patrick, we'll be fine."

"I'm not going to argue about this one, Aisha. It's dark out and getting late. Humor me."

"But we go places in the evening all the time and you're not there to follow us home so—"

He shook his head, firm in his stance. "Humor me, love. Please."

The firm resolve on his face would have been irritating if he hadn't called her *love* again and gotten her all confused. The first thing to come to her mind was to tell him not to call her that. But then she glanced at his earnest face with that determined square jawline and her heart had the nerve to do a double beat and she only wanted to hear him call her *love* again.

"Fine. But it's really not necessary."

She started up her car and after a short drive she was parking in front of the four-story apartment building where she and Dillon lived. She fully expected to see Patrick drive on by and maybe beep on the way. But nope, there he was, parking his SUV and getting out.

"I'll walk you guys to your door and be on my way," he offered with a smile.

"You really don't have to do that, Patrick."

"Mommy, I have to go to the bathroom." Dillon started hopping from one foot to the other.

"Okay, sweetie." She didn't have time to belabor the point with Patrick. So she let him walk them to the door.

As soon as they got there and she opened it, Dillon darted in and took off toward the bathroom. She stared after her child for a moment before turning to Patrick.

Patrick, who even after she had refused his date, was somehow, miraculously standing at her front door at the end of what felt like a date, even though her son had been with them.

Yes, she needed to have a word with this trickster. The way he operated, it would only be a matter of time before she was dating him.

"Can you come in for a minute? We need to have a little chat."

He glanced around from side to side and then behind him before pointing to himself. "You want *me* to come in?"

Funny guy. "Yes. Just for a minute. Please."

Chapter 7

He followed her into the living room after she shut the front door. He looked around her home and nodded.

"Nice place. It's really homey. I like it."

She smiled because she had worked hard to make the small space cozy for her and her son. She had caught clearances at Pier 1 and IKEA for most of the furnishings and knickknacks, and she had even picked up a few gently used finds at the Salvation Army and some consignment shops. The apartment had a lived-in, eclectic but stylish feel to it. And she credited the amateur decorating skills she had gotten when she was addicted to HGTV before she found the Food Network and discovered her true dream passion. But she couldn't let Patrick's compliments throw her off course. He was good, but he wasn't that good.

She took a deep breath and firmed her resolve. She saw where this was going. She had to nip this in the bud here and now. "Thanks. Have a seat."

Just as they took seats opposite each other on the tan-and-rust striped sofa and love seat set, Dillon came dashing into the living room.

"Can I watch TV?"

She shook her head. As much as she drummed into his head the difference between *can* and *may,* her child refused to use them properly.

"No you *may* not. But you *may* go read a little bit before bedtime. And when I come in to tuck you in we'll read a little more from Harry Potter."

A look of horror flashed across her Dillon's face. "M-o-m!" He glanced at Patrick and then marched his little feet over to her and whispered in her ear. "Not in front of Patrick. He'll think I'm a baby." He turned toward Patrick. "My mom is only kidding. She doesn't tuck me in or read me stories or anything like that."

"Oh, of course not. Big guy like you, being tucked in? I knew right away your mom was joking. But I'll tell you what. If you mom is like my mom—and they are both teachers so, I'm thinking she probably is—then she can probably tell a great story. My mom taught for years before she became an administrator. And when she read stories to us, she did all the sounds and painted the images from the books so well that my brothers and I thought we were in the story. And I'll let you in on a secret. I was a pretty big guy myself before I started feeling a little too old to listen to my mom read to me."

Dillon stared at Patrick. "How old were you when you stopped?"

"Well, now that depends on how you look at it. See, I have a little toddler niece named Cee Cee and two little nephews, Joel Jr. and Jason Jr., who are both crawling around wreaking havoc. My mother reads to them all the time. And sometimes, I hang around and listen. In fact, I just listened to her reading to Cee Cee the other day. 'Hansel and Gretel'—my favorite."

Dillon laughed, and oddly enough she found herself joining in. Soon the three of them were cracking up, just as they had been in the restaurant. And there was that feeling again, that easy, happy-family feeling she knew she shouldn't be experiencing.

Yes. It was time to nip this in the bud. She had to cut it off cold before she started believing it could go somewhere.

"Okay, Dillon. I need to talk with Patrick for a minute and then I'll be back there to...uh...check on you."

"Okay, Mom. G'night, Patrick."

"Good night, son. I'll see you again soon."

See, that was the problem! He shouldn't be making promises to her son that he wasn't going to keep. And he wasn't going to be able to keep them because she couldn't afford to let him keep them. Because if she let him keep them, then he'd be around all the time. And if he were around all the time, then she would never be able to continue resisting him. And she couldn't risk her heart any more on some dominant man who took up all the air in the room just by virtue of being there. So he had to go.

"Listen, Patrick, it's obvious that my son likes you a lot and—"

"Smart kid. He seems to be a great judge of character."

"Yeah…right… Anyway, the thing is, I can't have you making promises to him and raising expectations that you're not going to be able to meet. His father is already a major disappointment—"

"The man must be an idiot to disappoint a kid like Dillon."

"Yes, he is an idiot. Among other things…" *Mean, self-righteous, arrogant, cruel, a class-A-jerk…* She could think of so many descriptions for her ex-husband. "That's not the point, though. The point is—"

"I'm not him." Patrick sat up straighter in his chair and there was that confident, assured swagger that he wore like a favorite shirt.

"I know that. I never said you were. I—"

"I'm *not* him. I would never do anything to hurt you or Dillon."

She sucked her teeth. "Stop interrupting me. Let me finish making my point."

He shook his head. "Your point isn't based on facts. It's based on your fears. And I can help put your fears to rest. Because I am not him and I would never hurt you."

"You can say that all you want. But the fact is, we don't know that, do we? We can't see into the future and there are no guarantees."

"Your fear is going to make you miss out on magic, love."

"Magic?" She gave a nervous laugh. "I think you

might be thinking a little highly of yourself, don't you? And stop calling me *love*. I didn't give you permission to give me a nickname."

He chuckled. "I'm not thinking highly of myself. I'm thinking highly of *us* and what we can be together. I know I became a believer the moment I first set eyes on you. What's it gonna take for you to become a believer, too?" He paused and looked her dead in the eyes with a sincerity that startled her. "And I can't stop calling you *love*."

She folded her hands across her lap to fight the sudden impulse she had to fan herself. This was not going the way she had planned.

He had it so right and so wrong at the same time. She wasn't afraid of much of anything anymore and she certainly didn't fear him. But there was one thing she was deathly afraid of and that was his little nickname for her. Those four letters scared her more than anything. And she hated the clammy, out-of-control feeling that came over her when she even thought about risking her heart.

"Why don't you take a chance? What are you afraid of? I'll tell you what. How about you give me a month just to get to know you and Dillon. No strings. I'll take Dillon to the games, as I promised. Practice his pitching. We can even check out some museums and maybe the zoo. You don't have to be alone with me and we don't have to explore a relationship. We can just take it slow."

Urgggh! He was not making this easy at all. If she were still in her twinkling twenties and believed in love and half the things men said to get women to let down their guard, she would have had him in the bedroom already. He was good at running his game. She had to give him that.

She just stared at him, trying to think of a comeback that would get him to give up his attempted seduction of her. She had nothing. And he was so handsome sitting there on her sofa. Even in his relaxed pose, he exuded more masculinity than should comfortably fit in her small apartment. His muscles filled out that brown cotton shirt like nobody's business. And she wasn't even going to touch what those hulking thighs and that tight behind did to those jeans…

Luckily the phone started ringing, and that would buy her a little more time. She got up and looked at the caller ID. It was her parents' number and her heart stopped beating for a moment. They never called her. The only thing she could think of was that something must have happened to her mother. Her father must have finally… She couldn't even finish the thought.

"Excuse me, Patrick, I have to take this."

He nodded and she picked up the phone.

"Mom?" She said hesitantly, hopping it was her mother.

"This is your father, Aisha. Your mother has been forbidden to call you. So why would you think it was her?"

Aisha rolled her eyes. She knew there would never be a day when any man could forbid her from talking to her own child. Thank goodness she was breaking the cycle.

"Hello, Dad." She couldn't fix her mouth to say it

was good to hear from him or any other normal pleasantry. "Mom doesn't call me. But when I saw your number on the caller ID, I could only assume it would have been Mom. I never expected you to call at all after—"

"After you foolishly went against my wishes, divorced your husband and moved to that godforsaken city?"

"What can I do for you?"

"I'm calling because it is time for you to get your head on straight and do what's right for your child and not your own selfish needs. William is very close to becoming partner at the firm. We are having a reception for some key clients, and all the partners are bringing their wives and children. If he were to secure this client, who is very big on family and family values, it would give me a stronger case to argue for him—"

"Dad, what does this have to do with me? I divorced Bill. We are no longer married. And I am certainly not going to pretend so that he can win some client. The man hardly makes time to visit his child and he barely pays the child support and alimony he fought so hard to get reduced. The man could care less if Dillon and I lived in a shack and you are calling here pleading his case?"

Her blood started to boil and bubble up under her skin and angry beads of sweat pebbled on her forehead. She forgot about everything in that moment, even her hard-won independence and new life. Funny how her father could break her down and bring her back to being a scared and angry little girl.

Daniel Foster was a formidable attorney and a hard-edged man. There was a time when he would at least have a smile and a "how's my little princess today" for her. But those days were long since past. From the time she was in her teens and dared to voice her opinion on how he spoke to her mother, he'd used the same hard demeanor with her, as well. She spent the rest of her time in high school and most of college trying to reclaim her space as daddy's girl and rarely did anything to upset her father until she divorced Bill.

She clasped the phone tightly and tried to get a grip. She was not a child. She was a woman, and she was in control of her own life.

"I am arguing his case because I was the one who told him to fight you on the child support and the alimony. I'd hoped that once you got a taste of struggle and what it takes to survive in the world without a man to support you, you would come to your senses and go back to your husband. I had no idea you could be this stubborn and childish—"

She bit back bile as she angrily cut her father off. "Father, I am never going back to your little protégé *William*. You and *Billy-boy* can forget that. And I would rather die than help him with anything, let alone secure some client for your firm. He is a horrible, abusive man and any father worth a damn would be helping his daughter stay away from him. In any case, I am seeing someone now, and I know he would have a problem with me even having this discussion. So, if you're done…"

"Who are you seeing? Some low-life scumbag from

Paterson? A drug dealer? Some common thief?" The derision in his voice made her skin crawl, and for a moment she wished she really were brave enough to risk her heart again and she really were seeing someone.

But that kind of bravery was going to take time, and she didn't have that time right now—not when she had to take the air out of her father's self-righteous little bubble.

"You mean like the people you and Bill defend and help keep out of prison? No, I don't deal with such people, professionally or otherwise. The man I'm seeing is a real-life hero." Her recent trip to the fire station crossed her mind and she smiled. "A fireman."

"A fireman?" Her father bit out a sharp bitter laugh. "A blue-collar worker? Why not just date the garbageman?"

"There is nothing wrong with folks making an honest living." She should have known she couldn't win with her father. The man was a snob to the core and just plain mean to boot.

"Says the broke schoolteacher. Stop being an idiot and go back to your husband, princess."

"Don't call me princess! In fact, father, please do not call me again!" She hung up the phone, let out an angry half grunt, half yell and stamped her foot.

She wanted to throw the phone against the wall, but she knew that wouldn't solve anything. Plus her father's little *broke schoolteacher* swipe wasn't far off the mark. There certainly wasn't any money in her budget for a new phone.

"So, you're seeing a fireman, huh? A real-life hero?"

She jumped and clutched her chest at the sound of Patrick's voice. How had she let her father's irritating request make her forget that Patrick was in the room?

Oh, brother…

She shook her head and sat down on the sofa. Then she started to laugh and buried her head in her lap. Otherwise she'd cry.

What a night! What an un-freaking believable night.

"You're right, though," Patrick said as he joined in on her laughter. "Your new man…the fireman…he wouldn't like you even thinking about going anywhere with that idiot ex-husband of yours."

She really started laughing then and had tears running down her face by the time she was finished. Finally she sat up, holding her laugh-sore stomach as she did.

"Okay, before you get all crazy, I forgot you were in the room. My father makes me so angry. The nerve of him. If I had remembered you were actually in the room, I would have picked another fake boyfriend."

He clutched his heart in mock pain. "Oh…please tell me you're not *fake* breaking up with me already."

"Dear John…it's not you…it's me…" She painted on an expression of mock sincerity and tilted her head.

He closed his eyes and fell back on the love seat. "Oh, no! Not Dear John."

She hadn't laughed this hard in years and she suddenly wanted to laugh that hard again and again. She'd forgotten how good it felt. She could let him take out Dillon and her a few times. What could it hurt?

"Okay, seriously, though. I think it would be okay if

you, Dillon and I got to know each other. I'm not making any promises. Because I don't know that I'll be able to get into a relationship, or even go out on a real date with you. But Dillon seems to really like you and you're right—he is a good judge of character. So we'll see."

He nodded. "That's all I want—a chance. I promise you won't regret it."

She sucked her top lip into her mouth because she didn't trust what might have come out of her mouth at that moment. She'd already said way too much. So she just nodded, too. And she hoped like hell she wouldn't regret taking this chance.

Chapter 8

Patrick entered his one-family colonial home pretty much on cloud nine. He hadn't made as much progress as he had wanted to in terms of getting Aisha to trust him. But he had made more progress than he expected. And he knew... He now knew that there was no way he could give up.

He even found himself humming a little song as he entered his bedroom. He was taking off his shirt, ready to hit the sheets so that he could dream about Aisha. When he entered his bedroom, however, all humming and thoughts stopped.

What the hell is she *doing in my bed?*

"Hi, honey. I'm home." The scantly clad vixen stretched out on his comforter looked at him and let out a little Marilyn Monroe sigh.

"Courtney. What're you doing in my bed and how did you get in here?"

His ex-wife sat up in the bed and gave a fake pout. "So many questions… Can't we ask questions later…" She spread her legs and leaned forward. Her thong didn't cover anything, and he knew he would have to burn his sheets. "…After we get reacquainted? It's been too long, honey," she spoke in a fake lilting voice and purred.

She actually purred. *Who did she think she was? Catwoman? Good grief!*

He threw his head back at the ceiling. He only did it for a moment, though. Why she had picked this moment to show up was inconsequential. What he knew beyond a doubt was infinitely more important. He knew for damn sure he wasn't going to allow Courtney to get in the way of the relationship he hoped to build with Aisha.

"Put on your clothes and get out of my bedroom. We'll talk in the living room." He turned and left her there. If she wasn't out of the bedroom in ten minutes he was going to call either Lawrence or Jason and have her arrested. Hell, he still might call the cops and get her arrested for breaking and entering.

In approximately six minutes, she came sauntering out of the bedroom and slithered onto the couch right next to him.

He scooted over and turned to look at her. She still looked the same, stunningly beautiful and flawlessly made up. Her deep chocolate complexion and exotic features had always put him in mind of those beautiful high-fashion super models like Iman. Her skin was still smooth and tight. Clearly, the years had been kind to her. Even though she was the picture of beauty, he still couldn't figure out for the life of him what he ever saw in her.

"It's been too long, honey. I hope you're over your hard feelings now and we can pick up where we left off."

"You on drugs or something? Or are you just crazy? I'm no longer angry about the way things went down between us. But I'm also never going down that road with you again. Been there, done that, got the divorce papers in a pretty gold frame to celebrate the end of it." He stood up and started walking toward the door. "How did you get in here?"

"I found out where you keep the spare key and I let myself in." She crossed her legs as if to say she wasn't going anywhere anytime soon.

He turned and walked back over to her. "Aunt Sophie told you where I keep my spare key?" He held out his hand when he reached her. "Give me the key."

"Oh, come on, Patrick! This is ridiculous. It's been ten years. When. Are. You. Going. To. Forgive. Me." She stood up, put her hand on her hip and glared as she hissed out the words. Gone was the sultry vixen.

"It's been ten years, Court. I'm over you. I don't feel *anything* for you. I've moved on. And I'm involved with someone else now, someone I'm really serious about."

So maybe that was stretching the truth… He wasn't involved with Aisha, yet. But he was more than serious about her. He believed that a relationship with

Aisha was within his reach and he meant to bring it to fruition one day.

"What the hell did you think was going to happen? Did you think you were going to come over here, bat your eyes and…what? I'd take you back?"

She pouted again, this time for real. "You could take me back! What did I do that was so wrong that you had to cut me out for all this time? I said I was sorry. What ever happened to 'till death do us part,' huh? If you ever really loved me, you should have been able to forgive me. I forgave you."

This chick is crazy. She has lost her damn mind! "I didn't cheat on you!"

"But you left me alone for long periods of time. When you had time off, you hung out with your friends and your brothers. And you barely spent any time with me. Your stupid mother didn't like me, and the only person who ever paid any attention to me at all was your aunt." She became increasingly indignant as she ranted on. "And if she weren't trying to weasel her way back into the family home once it was passed down to you, she probably wouldn't have been concerned about me, either. I think you owe me an apology, Patrick Hightower. And I'm going to be your worst nightmare until you give it to me!"

She flung the key at him, swung her head so that the long jet-black weave did a swish and stomped out of the house.

He ran to the front door and yelled, "They'll be ice-skating in hell and the devil will be wearing a snowsuit before I'll ever apologize to you, Court. You are the one who wrecked the marriage. Grow up and deal with it. And don't you ever call my mother out of her name again! Stay the hell away from me. If you break into my place again, I'm pressing charges."

Courtney turned around, rolled her eyes, stuck out her tongue and flipped him the bird.

Lunatic! What the hell did I ever see in this crazy chick?

Slamming the door in disgust, he could only be glad that he had been alone when he came home. Aunt Sophie was going to learn how to stay out of his business. And he was never keeping a spare key under the flowerpot on the back deck again.

He plopped down on the couch and thought of Aisha and Dillon and the laughter they had shared that afternoon and evening. He thought of Dillon's description of one of Aisha's attempts at making a shepherd's pie based on the recipe she had gotten from one of her beloved cooking shows, and he started laughing even harder.

He realized then and there that nothing could ruin the high and the joy he got just from hanging with them for one day. And he knew nothing and no one was going to get in the way of him experiencing more joy. Not his ex-wife or Aisha's ex-husband.

No one.

"You said he would be happy to see me!" The ungrateful, sobbing girl poked Sophie in the chest and crowded her. Sophie had no idea the girl could be so aggresive.

"You said he wasn't seeing anyone and he would take me back." Courtney poked her again. "I made a fool of myself because of you, old lady. And I also left some good prospects in Trenton because you made me think there was a chance for me to reconcile with Patrick. So you had better fix this." She poked her again and Sophie fell onto her pink-and-green floral Queen Anne-style sofa.

Sophie clutched her pearls and took deep breaths. She shouldn't have let Courtney into her apartment. But how was she supposed to know that the girl had gone stark-raving mad?

"It would behoove you to keep your hands to yourself, Courtney! Then, I suppose if you could have done that in the first place we wouldn't be in this predicament, now would we?"

"Oh, you got jokes?" Courtney leaned forward and poked Sophie in the chest again.

Where did this violent person come from? Sophie wondered.

"We'll see how much you're laughing when I tell your entire family about how you were trying to use me to get into that house. Patrick is already seeing someone else, so you might as well start sucking up to her. Who knows, if Patrick can manage to make a woman happy long enough, he might just start a family and come into that house sooner than we think. But if you expect me to cover for you, you'd better believe that something has to be in it for me."

Sophie took a deep breath, composing herself and trying to come up with a way to salvage the situation.

"Patrick is not seeing anyone. Don't you think if he were seriously seeing someone, I'd know about it? My nephew and I are very close. He would have told me. He probably just told you that to lash out because he's still hurt by your betrayal. Tell me what happened and don't leave a word out."

Courtney went on an angry frustrated rant about what happened when she had gone to Patrick's home.

Sophie wanted to know who in the world told the girl to get darn near naked and place herself in the man's bed? Didn't she see that those whorish ways wouldn't get her anywhere?

Maybe she isn't the right one for this job after all...

But who else could she get? Time was passing and she wasn't getting any younger. It would be nice to be at peace and to go out in the same home she had come into the world in. And Lord knows it was way past time for that two-faced, fraud sister-in-law of hers, Celia, to be out of the Hightower home.

She listened to the tale Courtney told and became increasingly horrified. "You told him that I told you where the spare key was?"

"Well, you did," Courtney snapped.

"You're just messing everything up, Courtney. First of all, you shouldn't have tried to win him over with sex. Have you ever known a Hightower man to have his head turned by such common actions? They have women offering them that all day, every day. You're going to need some better tricks than that, young lady."

"I shouldn't need any tricks! He should be glad I even want him back, after the way he treated me."

Lord, the poor child is delusional.

"Do you want him back or not?"

"I want him back. But he is going to have to pay for treating me so rudely."

Delusional. Sophie shook her head.

This was her only shot at besting Celia once and for all. And she needed to have the last laugh. So Courtney would have to do. She only hoped the girl hadn't ruined everything beyond repair. "What are you doing for Thanksgiving?"

"You mean she showed up at your house when you weren't home, let herself in and proceeded to get undressed while she waited?" Lawrence frowned as he stretched. "You should have pressed charges. Wait— don't tell me you still have feelings for the woman. What about the nun?"

"I hope you changed the sheets?" Joel shuddered. "There ain't no telling where that skin has been."

Looking at his two brothers, he almost wished that he hadn't asked them to meet him at the gym this morning. He knew they were going to have jokes.

"Anyway, clown one and clown two. Aisha is not a nun. And I'm working on that. I'm making slow progress, but I am making progress. And I did change the sheets, threw those bad boys out, as a matter of fact. But that's not why I asked you guys to meet me here this morning."

"Yeah, I know. You wanted my help to get you in shape so that you can woo your schoolteacher." Lawrence stood up and stretched some more. "So whaddya want to start with—some hoops? Wanna hit the track a couple of times? Want me to spot you on the weights? What're you pressing?"

"He doesn't want help getting in shape. He wants help reviving his old-school playa skills. Being an original playa from the Himalayas is played out now, huh? You wanna learn from a new-school playa who has turned in his playa card but left the game so much better than he found it. Someone like your younger brother… Me." Joel popped his collar and grinned.

"Umm…" Patrick turned to Lawrence. "No, and…" he turned to Joel. "Hell. No." He shook his head. "I asked you here because I knew after I told you about the stunt Courtney pulled you'd go running to tell your wives. So I wanted to let you know that you are *not* to tell Samantha and Minerva, also known as Betty and Wilma or, my favorite, Ethel and Lucy, anything about what I just told you. Those two will be up in that book club running their mouths to Aisha about this the first chance they get."

"I'm wounded that you don't think I'd keep your secret, brother. Wounded, I say." Joel clutched his chest with his hand and chuckled.

"And I think you need to apologize not only to us, but to our wives." Lawrence shook his head and laughed. "And from what I heard, they gave you valuable information that allowed you to spend the weekend with the woman and her son."

"How in the… You know what, never mind. Just be sure to keep the information about Courtney to your-selves. And while we're on that subject, was that woman always crazy? What in the world did I see in her?"

"You were young and dumb, bro. Young and dumb," Lawrence offered and he pat him on the back.

"And yes, that chick was always crazy. Even Mama knew that," Joel added.

"What do you mean Mama knew that? Mama told me, 'If I liked it, she loves it,' when I told her I was marrying Courtney."

Both Joel and Lawrence burst out laughing.

Joel caught his breath first, only to start laughing again.

Lawrence finally stopped and clutched his stomach as he spoke. "Man, don't you know 'If you like it, I love it' is Mama talk for she can't stand the crazy woman?"

"Hmm… Courtney said Mama never liked her." Patrick rubbed his chin in thought.

"Well, Courtney at least got that right. Mama might not have tried to sabotage the relationship the way Aunt Sophie tried with all of us, except you and Courtney, but Mama didn't care for Courtney. The difference between Mama and Aunt Sophie is Mama will let you lead your life and love who you love. Aunt Sophie will meddle," Lawrence said.

"And now that Aunt Sophie has her favorite girl for you back in town, you'd better watch out. She'll have your relationship with Aisha derailed before it can even get on track for good. Keep your guard up," Joel advised. "Aunt Sophie can be very vindictive. I still haven't forgiven her for what she put Samantha through with her job. And let's not forget the hell she gave Penny. You can't let Aisha become another casualty of Hurricane Sophie."

"Oh, I won't. Trust and believe I won't. Aunt Sophie would want to tread lightly." Patrick ran his hand across his head. "Let's shoot some hoops."

He had always loved his aunt, and sometimes he felt as if he were her favorite. But there was no way he was going to let her mess up his barely formed relationship with Aisha. It was too precious to him already.

Celia Hightower stared at her sister-in-law for a full minute before opening the door and letting her in. She certainly wasn't expecting the woman to show up at her door today. There was no one home but her, and Sophie usually saved her torture for crowds. Ever since she had almost gotten Joel's wife Samantha fired from her job, they had banned her from family events. And she had pretty much stayed away, until now....

"What do you want, Sophie?" She led her into the living room and sat down.

Sophie sat on the sofa with her handbag on her lap, her shoulders reared back and her large, conelike breasts pointing out. The older woman's smooth mahogany complexion probably made it hard for people to tell her age with accuracy, but her stuffy, stuck-up demeanor always made her appear older than her years.

"I want to let bygones be bygones. I'm not getting any younger and neither are you. It's time we put this behind us—you and me. I'm tired of not feeling welcome in my family home, the home I was born and raised in. And I'm tired of my brother choosing your side over mine. So I'm going to give you all another chance. I'm going to come to Thanksgiving dinner. I've decided to forgive you all for the way you all treated me."

Unbelievable.

The woman would try the patience of a saint. And no matter how nice people thought Celia was, she knew her own limits and a saint she was not. In fact, she knew she probably shouldn't have opened the door for Sophie at all. Something inside her snapped, looking at Sophie's smug, self-righteous face.

"First of all, Sophie, you don't have anything to forgive. You brought everything on yourself. And you have been staying away because we banned you, not because you are trying to punish us. And if you think you're punishing us somewhere in that twisted little mind of yours, then you need to get a reality check because nobody is suffering from you not being around. In fact, it is only when you come around that the suffering begins."

Sophie took a big huff of air and reared up in her seat.

"Oh, poor, useless, delusional Celia. I have to give it to you, the sex you trotted out to turn my brother's head must have been good. He stayed with you this long after the boys have grown up and moved out. You really ought to give other social-climbing gold-diggers advice."

Celia jumped up from her seat and walked over to Sophie. No. She really shouldn't have let the woman in. That had been a mistake. This was not going to end well. She tried counting to ten and gave up at five. Celia's patience and her trying to keep the peace through the years had only made Sophie meaner.

It was finally time for a different tactic.

"I'm delusional? Sophie, what exactly did I marry your brother, the rookie cop, for, if not love? He wasn't rich. And for years when I was assistant superintendent in the Paterson public schools, I made the majority of our income. I'm the one with the degree. I'm my own woman and I was well on my way to becoming that woman before I married your brother."

Sophie rolled her eyes and let out a disgusted snort, her dark brown eyes flashing in indignant anger. "Thanks to me, Celia! I mentored you when your foster parents couldn't give a damn. I made sure you applied to college and for scholarships. I made sure you got my sorority's scholarship. I even stood up for you when my brother kept trying to prove that you were in a gang and unworthy of my time and attention. And how did you repay me? By marrying him. My baby brother."

"Your baby brother was a grown man and he made his own decisions, Sophie. I didn't make him marry me."

"You think he would have married you if your stupid behind hadn't gotten pregnant?" Sophie leaned forward with an angry glare. "Do you think he would have stayed with you if you hadn't nearly lost it when little

James Jr. was stillborn? That baby being born like that was the perfect out—"

She couldn't let Sophie finish her spewing. Celia reached back and smacked the woman with everything she had in her. Sophie's head bounced and her bun came loose.

"You hit me!" Tears sprang to Sophie's eyes, but Celia couldn't be concerned about that.

Her own eyes were flowing and her hot anger refused to stay under wraps. She hauled off and smacked Sophie again and the woman's purse went toppling on the floor.

"Don't you ever let my child's name fall out of your mouth again, Sophie! The stress of being a newlywed, finishing my degree and you and your mother, God bless the dead, contributed to my unhealthy state during that pregnancy. And I promised myself from then on that I would never let you and your hatefulness get to me again. But you will never quit, will you?"

A harsh laugh escaped Celia's lips and she did everything she could not to slap Sophie again. She told herself that this was just the kind of thing that Sophie would run with and tell everyone. Celia told herself that she should rise above it. She swallowed back years of bile and moved away from her target.

"You're going to be sorry for this. We'll see whose side James takes now. I told everyone you were just a little ghetto hoodlum."

Celia turned around and started to smack her again. It was time for them to have it out once and for all.

"Celia, don't do it."

James. When did he get home? Who cares? I'm taking this bitch out.

Celia smacked Sophie again and had raised her hand to hit the woman again only to be stopped by James. He held her, even as she struggled to get free. She was tired of Sophie.

Tired.

"She brought up my child. I told her never to bring up my child again."

"Is this why you wanted me to come home and meet you here, Sophie? So I could catch you goading my wife into giving you the whupping you've been begging her to give you for years?"

"How can you take her side, James? How can you? Look at me. She hit me. She's no better than that little thug girl Lawrence married. And she's the reason all your sons married inappropriately."

Celia struggled all the more to break free, only stopping when she felt James's calming lips on her temple.

"She's not worth it, babe. Sophie, you need to leave now. And until you can treat my wife and the rest of the women in this family with respect, you should stay away. You're my sister and I love you dearly, but I refuse to allow you to terrorize my wife."

"But I came to bury the hatchet and to try and make peace before the Thanksgiving holiday. I wanted to make peace with both of you. And she attacked me." Sophie wiped the tears from her eyes and for a brief moment Celia remembered her former mentor as a friend, the woman who—like it or not—had helped change her life for the better.

And just like that, the memory was gone. That woman was gone, and this evil, hateful creature was in her place.

"If you call *making peace* bringing up my deceased child and blaming me for it, then you need a lesson in peacemaking." She felt her husband stiffen at her words. She hated that Sophie made her remind him of that bleak time in their lives. He had had to bury his first son, his namesake, almost alone because she had been so overcome with grief that she had almost lost her grip on reality.

After coming that close to losing her mind, and after getting help for her severe postpartum depression she had found a way to deal with Sophie and her mother-in-law. She made her husband choose. And it was only after his mother passed away and he hadn't been able to say goodbye that she realized she couldn't deny him his family, as crazy as they were. And she allowed Sophie back into their lives. She had turned the other cheek time and time again, and it had still come down to this.

"Sophie, if you really want to be forgiven, if you really want peace, then you had better never mention James Jr. again. You need to watch the things that come out of your mouth, because I can't promise I won't wipe the floor with you if it happens again. You can come to Thanksgiving dinner. But you have been warned." Celia let her words linger before turning to leave.

James could deal with his sister now. She was too tired to do so. And something told her she would need all her strength for whatever Sophie was cooking up.

Sophie touched her jaw as she eyed her brother. James was going to take Celia's side. Sophie could tell.

She hadn't expected the little fool to actually hit her.

From the day Celia married James and became a Hightower, she had pretty much tried to keep the peace, and she had never confronted Sophie. Maybe she had finally had enough… Well, she wasn't the only one. Sophie had had enough, too.

Sophie let out a nervous chuckle. "I guess you were right all those years ago. She is a little gang—"

"Do not talk about my wife, Sophie." James glared at her as he cut her off. "All these years, she has tried to make things work and tried to give you a chance to change your evil ways—"

She had never seen her brother so angry and he had certainly never called her anything as harsh as *evil*. She had to cut him off. "Evil! I—"

He wouldn't let her defend herself. He cut her off. "Sophie, enough! *Enough is enough.* She is my wife! She has given me five children. And for you to bring up the child who died, when you know that she has never really gotten over it all these years is cruel, even for you! You need to leave. And if you can't get it together and be civil on Thanksgiving, don't feel like you have to show up, even though Celia extended the olive branch and invited you. This is your last chance, sis. You went too far this time."

"But she hit me! What about that?" Her indignation would not be contained.

"Go home, Sophie. Go home and think about the place you want to have in this family. Your nephews are already close to cutting you off. You have a great-niece and two great-nephews and a new baby on the way. This family is happy. My sons have married some wonderful women and I'm proud of them. I can't stand by and let you terrorize the family any longer."

Sadly, there she had it. James was just too far gone to be of much use. But Patrick had always been her favorite nephew anyway. And Courtney...although she had surprised her by poking her that way...was just malleable enough for Sophie to influence. There might be hope for her yet. Getting Celia out of the family home before Sophie died was worth anything Sophie had to do, anyone she had to sacrifice. Celia was going to pay for the personal suffering her betrayal had caused Sophie all these years. If it was the last thing Sophie did, Celia was going to pay.

Chapter 9

Aisha placed the vase full of pink, white and red roses on the windowsill of her classroom, right next to the other four vases. She had gotten a vase a day since Monday on and they all had the same note. "Please go out on a date with me." And each card had a number that she assumed was either Patrick's cell phone or home number.

She opened the latest card expecting to see the same message, but instead it said.

Love,

    I have three tickets to see the Giants on Saturday and I know one really cool kid who would love to go. I'm hoping his mom will come with us and we can make a day out of it. And before you say no because you don't date, know that this is not a date. It is me and you and Dillon hanging out and getting to know one another. When we go out on a date—and we will one day—you'll know it. I'll stop by at noon on Saturday and if you and Dillon are outside and ready to go, I'll take that as a yes… Hope to see you on Saturday, Patrick

She closed her eyes and exhaled.

Patrick Hightower was relentless, and she barely had any resolve left. She looked at the wide-eyed children in her class.

"She's going to cry. My mommy always cries when my daddy gives her flowers." Michaela nodded her head as she spoke, all the while looking and waiting for the predicted tears.

"Can we have some of those flowers, Ms. Miller? You gonna leave them here all weekend? They gonna get cold and die." Lizzy eyed the flowers longingly.

Some of the other students nodded in agreement with their classmate.

"Yes, Ms. Miller, what're you going to do?" Toni asked with a big grin on her face. She was worse than the kids.

Aisha crossed her eyes at her friend and teaching assistant. "I don't know. But I do know one thing, it's story time."

"Yay!" The round of voices bounced off the walls as the children got out of their seats, grabbed pillows for the floor and jockeyed for the position closest to her chair.

She grabbed a book from the many children's books on the shelf and sat down to read to her class. She hoped it would take her mind off a certain firefighter, and couldn't help but laugh when she got a look at the cartoon fireman on the cover of the book.

So much for that plan… Everything in the universe seemed to be pointing to Patrick Hightower.

The rest of the day went along pretty uneventfully. She decided to share her flowers with her students, giving each of them two to take home. She gave Toni a vase and took a vase home herself and there were still flowers left in the classroom. Patrick Hightower certainly knew how to wear a girl down.

She picked Dillon up from his after-school program and thought about what she'd cook for dinner. Keeping it simple was always her strong point. But she was tired of baked chicken and baked pork chops and baked salmon.

She was tired of playing it safe.

And she had just seen a really great recipe on TV the other day that was sure to knock Dillon's little socks off if she got it right. She had most of the ingredients in the apartment, too. She figured she could improvise the rest.

She thought she would be able to pull it off, but, judging by the way Dillon swallowed and then took a big gulp of juice after he'd tasted it, she hadn't succeeded. She looked at Dillon's sweet little face as he tried to eat the thirty-minute version of coq au vin and not hurt her feelings and she gave in.

"Is it that bad, sweetie? I thought I had it this time. The

recipe looked *so-oo* easy. I just knew I could do it." She took Dillon's unfinished plate and emptied it in the trash.

"You make the best baked chicken and rice, Mom. I love when you make that." He was trying to make her feel better. She really had the world's greatest kid.

"But I make that all the time. Don't you get tired of eating baked chicken, baked macaroni and cheese, baked ziti, baked blah, blah, blah." She looked at the brown glob on her plate and threw that in the trash, too. "Oh, well, how's about I call Frank and Joe's and we have some *baked* pizza delivered?"

"I think that's a great idea, Mom!" Dillon offered with a giggle.

Her heart swelled just looking at him. Suddenly, she remembered Patrick's note. Dillon deserved to go to the Giants game. Even if she couldn't work her way around to agreeing that she deserved to go out on a date and have fun with the fine, sexy fireman, she could let her son experience a real professional football game and take the chance to get to know Patrick a little better. She had made a deal with him that she would, after all.

"So, sweetie, how would you feel about going to a Giants game tomorrow with Patrick? He asked if we wanted to—"

"Yes! Yay! I can't wait! They're playing the Patriots tomorrow. Awesome!"

The gleeful expression on his face made any potential risk she was taking with her heart worth it. Dillon's happiness had been all that mattered to her for so long. But the light, airy feeling in her heart let her know without a doubt that Dillon wasn't the only one happy about the prospect of seeing Patrick tomorrow.

By the time there was a knock on her apartment door, she had to admit that she was a little more than hungry. She was probably going to eat more than her fair share of the pepperoni pizza they had ordered. She rushed to open the door without looking through the peephole and instantly regretted it.

Her father must have made a call to his protégé puppet. Because her ex-husband stood at her door and he hadn't darkened her doorstep in years, not even to see his son.

She stared at him. His toasted-cinnamon complexion was ruddy with anger, as usual. His jet-black curly hair was cut low so that the curls formed deep waves. He was growing a mustache and it seemed to cover up his thin lips. With his tall, medium build and refined features, most women would probably find him handsome. After being married to him and now blissfully divorced from him, she wasn't one of those women.

"What are you doing here, Bill?"

He pushed past her and made his way into the apartment. "I don't need a reason to be here since my hard-earned money is helping to pay for this dump." He glared back at her. "Shut the door. We need to talk and you're going to listen."

The pizza delivery guy showed up at that moment. So she handed him the money and took the pizza. It gave her just enough time to compose herself, temper her anger and gather her courage. Just for safe measure, she left the front door ajar.

"You can wait in the living room, Bill. I'm going to get Dillon set with his dinner and then I have five minutes to spare for whatever you need to discuss." She called for her son, who came immediately running out of his room and down the narrow hallway.

"Yay! Pizza…" His voice trailed off when he saw Bill.

"Dillon, say hello to your father," she coached her son. She couldn't blame the kid for being too surprised to speak. He probably had forgotten what the man looked like.

"Hi, Dad," Dillon mumbled.

"Hey, kid." Bill glanced at his watch and then glared at her.

Aisha rolled her eyes. She would always regret that she hadn't picked a better man to procreate with. Although she lucked out and ended up with the best kid in the world, it broke her heart to see him hurt by Bill's callous actions and attitude.

She set Dillon up at the kitchen table and gave him a kiss on the forehead. "Mommy will be back to join you in a minute as soon, as she's done seeing what he wants."

She took a deep breath and then walked into the living room where Bill was sitting on the sofa, looking about as comfortable as the devil at a revival meeting.

"So, as I said before, what are you doing here?"

"I'm here because I heard you've really lost it. Now you have all kinds of strange men in here around my kid. And if you think that's going to fly with me, then you are sadly mistaken." He glared at her and she glared right back.

"Since when did you ever give a damn about my son?" She whispered between clenched teeth.

The nerve of this man!

"You've seen him what…three or four times in the last five years? You barely want to pay the measly child support you and your crooked lawyer friends, including my own father, worked out for you. You could care less. So, please, spare me."

"It's your fault that my son isn't in his nice home, enjoying all the luxuries a son of mine should have. He shouldn't be living in this hot mess, attending public school in this city with little future criminals in training. But his mother is a vindictive bitch who had a little hissy fit after one small situation between us that we could have worked our way—"

"You. Punched. Me. In. The. Face." The heat rose from her chest to her face and she could barely contain her outrage. How dare he belittle what he had done or her response to it?

"One time! We could have gotten past all that." He shrugged in a nonchalant manner. "You filed for divorce and I decided to let you see how hard your life would be taking care of a five-year-old without me or your father there to cater to your every whim."

"And I did just fine. I finished school, got a job and I'm taking care of my child. But, most important, my son doesn't have to live in a home where his father hits his mother and I don't have to worry about him becoming an abuser like you."

Bill's toasted cinnamon-complexion turned even

redder and she could tell that he was working hard to keep his anger in check. Although she was no longer afraid of him, she also didn't want him to lose it in her apartment.

"Your father wants us to try to work this out for his grandson's sake, and I need to make partner."

There it was. When she was a twenty-year-old college sophomore enjoying life away from home and finally free, her father decided that the hot new attorney at his firm would be the perfect man for her to marry. She'd been young and naive and a tiny bit enthralled by the twenty-seven-year-old's handsome looks. But she wasn't sure she was ready to get married. He father said women like her only went to school to get their MRS degree, and since he'd found the perfect man for her, she didn't need to finish college. She hadn't been strong enough to stand up to the pressure then. But she was more than strong enough now.

She took a deep breath and folded her hands in her lap. "My father doesn't care about his grandson any more than you do. My father likes to control people, probably even more than you do. He doesn't control me any longer. I already told him—and now I'm telling you—I'm not going to the reception your firm is having. And I most certainly am not in the running for a second round with you. It's over."

He leaned forward with a mean and vicious-looking smirk on his face. "You think you've done something special because you got a BA in elementary education and the Paterson public schools hired you to teach some five-year-olds? That's about the only thing your simple behind could do. It's a good thing you were blessed with that face and that body, or your father wouldn't have found anyone to marry you. You're lucky I was even considering giving you another chance."

"Take your second chance and you know exactly what you can do with it. And, for the record, if you were the best my father could come up with in his quest to marry me off, I wish he hadn't bothered at all. The only good thing to come from that wasted ten years of my life was my son."

"Fine." He smirked. "Have it your way. I want to start seeing *my* son. I'll be picking him up on weekends from now on."

"What?" Her heart jumped to her throat and she felt a slight dizziness overcome her. "You haven't been interested in seeing him before. Why now?"

"It doesn't matter." He gave another one of those nonchalant, devil-may-care shrugs and she wished she could smack him. "I have rights. I was granted visitation. And unless you want to take this back to court and see if the judge won't decide that I should actually have full custody, then you should just have my son ready next weekend. I have plans this weekend. But from now on, the weekends are mine."

Bill got up walked toward the door.

"Aren't you going to at least say goodbye to the son you suddenly just *have* to be able see?" She bit the words out through her barely controlled anger.

"You can tell him I said goodbye. Have him ready around this time next Friday. I'll be here to pick him up."

She followed him to the door and locked it. It felt as if she were on autopilot. The only thing she knew for certain was that she would do *anything* to protect her son.

Driving up to Aisha's apartment building and seeing her and Dillon standing outside, dressed and ready to go to the Giants game, made Patrick's heart nearly beat out of his chest. His throat tightened and his lungs suddenly felt overly full. He had tried not to get his hopes up, just in case she wasn't there, and seeing her nearly floored him.

They enjoyed the Giants game and surprisingly she didn't put up a fight when he'd suggested that they have dinner at Dave and Buster's and play some games while they were there.

She was strangely unlike herself and he could tell that something was bugging her. Rather than hound her about it and spoil the good time, he decided to wait and see.

After a while the thrill of playing video games wore off on the two adults and they decided to just follow Dillon around and watch him play game after game after game.

"I could get used to this. Look at him. He's so excited." Patrick let the words fall out of his mouth before he could stop them.

Aisha stared at him for a moment without saying a word. "It probably wouldn't be a good idea to get used to it."

"Why not? Am I that bad that you really can't see

trying to build something real with me?" He cursed the fact that he couldn't just be nonchalant and coast with this woman. He couldn't act as if he didn't care. Because he did care—a lot.

Aisha watched Dillon fake speed racing on the Indy 500 game. And Patrick watched her. He focused on every feature of her pretty brown face, every strand of her black hair.

"My ex-husband showed up at our house last night. After years of canceling visitation and basically ignoring his son, he wants to have him on the weekends." A tear escaped her eye and she angrily wiped it away.

Patrick let out the breath he'd been holding. So that was it… Her ex was trying to work his way back into the picture? Was there something in the water that was causing ex-wives and ex-husbands to trot their happy behinds back out? Why couldn't they just stay gone?

"So do you think you would ever take him back? Is that where this is heading?" He had to know. Better to have the news kill him now than later. He was already in too deep.

She let out a sharp laugh. "That will *never* happen. He's an abusive jerk, and I will never subject myself to that again."

"He hit you?" The hairs on the back of his neck stood up, and he suddenly had the urge to find her ex and do him bodily harm.

"Once. And then I divorced his behind. But he was verbally abusive for years and I'm still angry at myself for staying as long as I did. And I will not have my son subjected to that crap. I'm thinking I'll just leave the state. Dillon and I will just find another place to live. Maybe the South, or the Midwest—I don't know. I just know I can't let him take my baby for a minute, let alone a whole weekend."

Dillon came running over to them and stopped short when he got in front of them. "Umm... I ran out of tokens..." He shuffled from foot to foot and eyed the tokens Patrick was holding in his hands. "You guys done playing?"

"Uh-uh, Dillon... I know you haven't used up all your tokens and now you're over here begging Patrick for his. You know you're wrong." Aisha laughed as she reached out and mussed her son's hair. "Here, child, take mine and leave Patrick alone."

Dillon reached for the tokens and took off for the next game. They walked right behind him, never taking their eyes off the hyperexcited kid.

"Wait up, Dillon," Patrick called.

Dillon spun around and took a step back toward them. Patrick held out his tokens and dropped them in Dillon's hands.

"All right! Thanks, Patrick!" He stopped at another kid-appropriate video game and started spending his newly acquired bounty.

As much as it killed him to have to be the one to try and talk some sense into Aisha, Patrick knew he had to try. And it really bugged him that he had to take her idiot ex-husband's side.

"Has he ever hit Dillon?"

"No! Thank God. I think I'd be in jail if he did. But he has hurt my baby emotionally. Do you know what it feels like to have a kid stop asking about his father? He has just given up on ever having Bill love him."

"So don't you think if Bill wants to finally step up and be a man and spend time with his son, you should let him? If you run away, you'll essentially be breaking the law, and denying your son something he apparently wants... His father's love." Patrick stopped and stared at her.

Her stubborn face was contorted in one of those you-can't-tell-me-anything expressions. She obviously wanted to tell him to mind his own business. But until she did, he fully intended to try to get her to see where the idiot Bill may have been coming from.

"Men can be dense sometimes, Aisha. We don't always get it right the first time out of the gate—"

"No way... You're kidding..." She widened her eyes in mock surprise and mumbled sarcastically.

"Ha, ha. Seriously, I know if I had a kid like Dillon, weekends wouldn't be enough. And a boy needs a dad. If his dad is finally stepping up, you should give him a chance to rebuild their relationship. If he drops the ball, we'll be there to pick it up. But you can't run from this." He turned to face her, watching her as she watched her son.

"What do you mean *we?*" She offered a smirk and then nibbled on her lower lip.

He decided to let her figure out what he meant on her own. She was a smart woman. She had to know that where they were headed was a point of no return.

"And I know you won't run, because the only thing

you're afraid of is *us*." He leaned forward and brushed her lips with his.

The electric shock of the momentary touch almost made his heart stop. When her little tongue darted out and touched her lips as if to savor where his lips had just been, it was all he could do not to kiss her again for real.

"Hey look, you guys. It's 'Dance Dance Revolution.' Mom's really good at this one. I have three tokens left." Dillon glanced back and forth between the video game and them.

"Oh, this will be good. Are you light on your feet, Mr. Big Burly fireman? Can you dance?" Aisha eyed him for a moment, looking him up and down. "Nah, I don't think so. Dillon, Patrick won't be able to hang. I think it's just you and me, kiddo."

"I think I've just been insulted. I'll have you know that I have moves. I will dance the two of you under the rug." Patrick couldn't believe she'd played him like that.

"A little less talk and a little more action. Come on, let's see what you can do." She reached out and took his hand.

The shock of her touch warmed him and he broke out in a grin. When she didn't let go, he squeezed her hand. She squeezed back.

Once they were back at her apartment and Dillon was in bed, Aisha let the events of the day swirl through her mind. She took a sip of her wine and stared at Patrick. How had she gone from not dating him to sitting in her living room sharing a nightcap with him? And how had such a big powerhouse of muscles like him managed to beat her and her ten-year-old son at "Dance Dance Revolution"?

She licked her lips as she thought about how smooth and agile the man was on that dance pad. He hadn't lied at all. He certainly had moves. She wondered what other kind of moves he had, and she licked her lips again.

This time, without any warning or announcement, Patrick swooped down and covered her lips with his. And this wasn't one of those soft, fleeting brushes he'd been priming her up with. No, this was a long, savoring, marking kiss.

She opened to his demanding mouth and let her tongue taste what it really wanted to taste. Him. She licked her full lips, giving as good as she got.

He pulled her off the sofa and onto his lap, continuing to devour her with his hot, scalding mouth. She had started something by licking her lips that he was clearly going to finish. All the places she had just licked were now covered by him, remarked and claimed as his territory and his alone. She felt her lips spread into a gleeful smile as his hands roamed her breasts. With just a few swipes of her nipples she felt herself coming undone.

Aisha felt overwhelmed. Never had a man been so attentive to her needs. She started to glimpse the gentle soul that was hiding behind the domineering persona and started to fear that she was already losing her heart to him. When he kissed her again, she knew for sure that she had already lost her heart. She halted the kiss and tried to catch her breath. It was time for her to be brave enough to claim some happiness for herself, if only for one night.

"Stay for a little while," she said as she took his hand and led him back into her bedroom.

She sat him on the foot of the bed and straddled his lap. This time, she covered his lips with hers, lightly brushing the way he'd done all those times before. He had her torn between telling him not to kiss her and begging for more.

But he was not going to let her just brush his lips. He wrapped his arms around her and held her tight, intensifying the kiss at the same time.

He stopped, gulped a large dose of air and stared at her. "Are you sure, Aisha? Because I want you to… No… I need you to be sure about this. This is too important. It means too much to me…. You have to be sure. Please be sure…"

She nodded.

"Love, I need you to say yes. I need to know you're sure. Because there won't be any going back from this, Ms.-I-don't-date."

He was giving her an out.

She smiled.

How had she managed to resist this man as long as she had? He had made her smile more in the short time that she'd known him than she had smiled the entire time she was married to Bill. Her taste in men had improved tenfold and Patrick Hightower was the proof.

"I want this. I want you. Do you want me or should I let you go home now?" She slowly trailed her tongue along her lips and he let out a low rumbling growl before pulling her onto the bed and covering her with his body.

He made quick work of her clothes and his, and she helped as much as she could until she realized that he didn't need any help. Her hands were just getting in the way of his progress and stopping him from doing what needed to be done.

He pulled out a condom and put it on. She watched and her eyes nearly bugged out of her head. He was unbelievably huge. She had only had one other lover before. She didn't know if Patrick would be able to fit. But she was certainly ready to try.

He slowly and lovingly entered her, inch by inch, stopping to allow her time to adjust and peppering her lips, her cheeks, her neck and her breasts with soft pecks along the way to make the invasion a little easier for her.

She let out a breath. She had never felt so full and he hadn't even entered her all the way yet. He continued to enter her slowly until he had reached the hilt. He then kissed her soundly, caressing her mouth with his as his hands caressed her body.

His hands squeezed her breasts. His finger flicked her nipples. He rubbed the flesh of her stomach and the small of her back. He let his hands span her hips and rest on her buttocks. He did all this touching without moving his hips, giving her plenty of time to adjust to his size and width.

She tentatively moved her hips, wiggling and grinding softly, letting him know that she was ready. He groaned before withdrawing and thrusting back in. Her breath caught at the power of his thrust. But she managed to move her own hips, meeting him and mating in the age-old dance until they both cried out in release.

Patrick got rid of the protection and then came back and held her in a spooning position. He couldn't believe what had just happened. He had never felt anything this close to perfect in all his life. He wanted to go on holding and caressing her until the end of time.

She wiggled her hips seductively and he could have sworn his skin heated to a sizzle. She was that hot. Together they were that hot. It was just as he'd said they would be. Magic.

He ran his fingers through her long hair and moved the sweat-soaked strands that had become stuck to her face. He kissed her neck, her cheek and then her delicious mouth.

"Thank you, love. Thank you for taking a chance on us. You won't regret it." He kissed her again, soundly. Her already plush lips were kiss-swollen to the point that they looked like they had had some kind of plumping injection in them.

"You're welcome." She wiggled her hips again and he felt himself rising yet again to the occasion.

He closed his eyes and willed his erection back down. He could tell that she hadn't been sexually active in a while, and he didn't want to do anything to hurt her or make her not want to do it again. He also didn't want to appear greedy.

She wiggled her hips again before turning around to face him. She pulled his face down to hers and nibbled on his lips. Her hand moved from his face, trailed his chest and then stroked his penis. Her loving strokes made him forget all his reasons for going slow and just cuddling. Before he knew it he had flipped her over, grabbed protection and entered her slowly from behind.

"Oh… Patrick…" She panted out his name as she pushed her buttocks back to meet the thrust of his pelvis. Each of his movements was met with one of hers.

Thrust. Push. Thrust. Push. Thrust. Push.

The rhythm of their lovemaking lulled him into a space where anything was possible. All kinds of things swirled through his head, things he wished he could say without scaring her or making her run for the hills.

He reached under her, caressed her breast with one hand and her clitoris with the other. She mewled and it was the sweetest, sexiest sound he had ever heard.

"I'm… Oh, God… I'm…" She mewled again.

He licked straight up her back before whispering in her ear. "Come for me, love."

He felt her body shake and convulse as she squeezed and tightened around him like a pulsating vise. That did it for him and he found it impossible to hold out on his own release. His eyes closed so tightly that he saw stars in the back of his head. His toes curled up and the muscles in his legs pulled to the point of cramping.

As they lay panting in the aftermath, he felt vindicated, confirmed, right, so many things. He had found the one and he wasn't letting her go.

Chapter 10

Watching her baby leave with Bill the following Friday darn near broke her heart. The worse part was, Bill seemed to get a kick out of her pain. The smug smirk on his face almost made her turn abusive. She would have paid money to smack it off him.

"Think about this while we're gone this weekend, Aisha. We can be a family again. You can bring your silly little behind back home where you belong." Bill curled up his lips in a sneer. "I'd marry you again if you could show me that you'd learned your lesson and your place. It doesn't have to be this damn difficult."

She glared at him and wanted to spit in his face. She then turned to her son, who was sitting in the front seat of Bill's BMW sports car.

"Be careful with my child this weekend, Bill. If anything happens to him, you will regret ever being born. And try to actually pay some attention to him. He's a great kid. If you take the chance to actually get to know him, you might—"

Bill's complexion reddened. "Shut up, Aisha. I don't need your advice on how to handle my son. You're getting really mouthy and opinionated these days."

She took a deep breath. "Bill, can't we handle this in a different manner? You weren't always like this—"

"You made me like this, Aisha. You shouldn't have left me after one mistake. I apologized, but you wanted to play hard. I came to you offering a chance to get back together and you still want to play hard. So I'm just showing you how the big boys play. Learn your position and maybe we can handle this in a *different manner.*" Bill smirked.

Then he got into his car and took off with her son. She stared after the car and wondered when he had turned into such a monster. Had he always been that way and had she been just too young and dumb to realize it? The tears started to fall almost immediately as she walked up the stairs and into her apartment.

After about an hour of sulking and drowning her sorrows in chocolate chip cookie dough ice cream, she decided to try to read the book club's selection. At least she could be ready for that when they met next week.

Once she was about halfway through the steamy novel, she regretted it. She found herself hot and bothered in the worst way. It never used to bother her before. She used to love to read the hot scenes.

That was before she knew what Patrick's hot kisses felt like. What he tasted like... What he felt like inside her. Now when she read the scenes all she could do was think of the many ways Patrick had contorted her body and made it sing. She felt so uninhibited when she was around him. It was like prim and proper Aisha had a wanton twin sister who came out whenever he touched her.

Just as she was ready to try to pick up the book again the phone rang. She marked her place and answered the phone.

"So, I was thinking that a certain sexy mom I know must be feeling a little bored right about now. Maybe bored enough to finally say yes to a date with a certain fireman. Do you think she's bored enough to say yes?" Patrick's smooth baritone met her as soon as she picked up the phone.

She grinned and answered without hesitating. "Yes."

"Yes?" Patrick repeated in a questioning and nonbelieving tone.

She laughed. "Yes. Now come get me and take me somewhere already!"

When he showed up about five minutes later, she was already downstairs and she wasted no time getting in his SUV.

"I can't believe you finally said yes," Patrick said.

"I said yes because you played dirty and were so nice to my son," she lied as if the night of passionate, steamy sex and the growing feelings she had for him had nothing to do with her affirmative response.

"You said yes because you have been wanting to say

it since day one, and you're so grateful I gave you the right excuse to follow your heart." He leaned forward and brushed his lips lightly against hers.

Her usually proper mouth had the nerve to part, wantonly so. And her tongue, usually tame and controlled, came dashing out, wild and searching. She found herself hungrily drinking from his mouth as if he had the fountain of life housed between his wonderfully thick, skilled and demanding lips.

Her teeth even got involved. What kind of scarlet woman uses her teeth when kissing? Why was she nipping on a man she barely knew while sitting in his car in front of her apartment at the beginning of the date? She could at least let him take her out first.

His arms pulled her closer until she was leaning uncomfortably over the stick shift. But did her body register one lick of discomfort? No. In fact, she called on some lost acrobatic skills in her gene pool and twisted around even more, so that more of her body could connect with the solid wall of muscle that was Patrick Hightower.

Why she didn't just get out of the car, walk over to the driver's side, open the door and just get in his lap was beyond her. It would have been the more pragmatic and reasonable thing to do. But who could think of pragmatic and reasonable when she was clearly drinking from a mouth that offered ambrosia?

She twinned her hands on either side of his chiseled cheeks and tried to contain him so that she could gracefully end the kiss. It would be hard, but she had to do it. She suckled none too gently and inhaled a great gulp of air as she pulled away.

His strong, masculine hand reached out and stroked her cheek as he gazed at her, his eyes gleaming with passion.

"Whatever the reason, love, I'm glad you finally said yes. And I'm going to do everything in my power to make sure that yes never turns to no."

Now was the time, right? Now was the time to bring her reasonable, nonwanton self back into perspective and clear up any misunderstanding her blatant display of lust might have triggered. But all she could do was let out a gasp of air and nod.

She nodded. She actually nodded, and she knew her treacherous eyes were saying yes to the fire captain. And she knew she was in a lot more trouble than she ever could have imagined.

They went out to dinner at a fancy Italian place in Paramus. It had been so long since she'd gone to a non-kid-friendly restaurant that she almost squealed with glee at the thought of white tablecloths and flickering candles.

"Thanks for calling and asking me out, Patrick. Thanks for being so persistent." She rubbed her hand over the tablecloth and smiled.

"How are you holding up? I know it must have been hard for you today."

"It was hard. It was also obvious that he could care less about spending time with Dillon. That's what hurts more than anything. Dillon's feelings get hurt each time his father rejects him."

"Have you thought about going back to court? It would be hard to get his visitation revoked since he wasn't physically abusive to Dillon. But maybe you can make the case about his neglect and—"

"He's already threatened to take me back to court and sue me for full custody. And with that team of sharks he works with—my father included—I wouldn't be surprised if they actually took my kid away. You should have seen how ugly the divorce was and how they fought me on the child support. No, I think it's best if I either take my kid and run, or let Bill get tired of spending his weekends with Dillon. I just hope he doesn't inflict too much damage in the interim."

She inhaled and exhaled as she shook her head. "Can we change the subject? I don't want to spend our first real date talking about Bill."

"Sure thing. How about we talk about what we are going to do afterward? Would you like to go check out a non-kid-friendly movie? I'm sure you're more than ready to see a film without animation. I was talking to Dillon and he's seen just about every kid flick that's come out in the past year."

"Yes, I've seen them all. And I would love to go check out a grown-up movie, but maybe tomorrow. Tonight, I don't want anything between us but sweat and latex."

Patrick's fork dropped and his mouth fell open. He recovered quickly though, and a slow seductive grin spread across his face as he signaled the waiter for the check.

They decided to go to his place, since his place was

closer to the restaurant. Once inside, they wasted no time with small talk. They began undressing at the door and barely made it to the living room with their underwear.

The sound of someone clearing her throat stopped both of them dead in their tracks. Mid-kiss they turned to see who it was.

The woman sitting on the sofa in a sexy short negligee and thigh-high boots made Aisha do a double take. She didn't know what kind of kinky stuff Patrick was into, but she *certainly* didn't get down like that.

"Who is *she?*" Aisha and the unnamed woman said in unison.

In addition to the silky negligee, the unnamed woman sported a thousand-dollar weave or lace-front wig or whatever manner of fake hair… Aisha just knew the woman hadn't been born with it.

Patrick cursed. "Courtney, I told you to stay away. I'm not interested in getting back together with you. *Ever.* I'm seeing someone." He pulled Aisha close. "How did you get in here? I didn't put the key back after you snuck in the first time."

His ex-wife. Courtney…

Aisha mentally replayed everything the women in the book club had said about the woman foolish enough to cheat on Patrick.

"I made copies! What are you doing with her? Sophie said you weren't really seeing someone or she would have known. I came to give you another chance." Courtney yelled and screamed with so much raw emotion and indignation one would have thought she was the wronged spouse or someone had broken into her home.

Aisha shook her head in disbelief. Between her vindictive ex-husband and Patrick's apparently crazy ex-wife, she and Patrick really knew how to pick them. What did that say about the new relationship they were embarking on together?

Patrick walked over to the cordless phone and picked it up. After dialing, even Aisha was surprised to hear the words that came out of his mouth.

"Yes, my name is Patrick Hightower and I live on 750 East 30th Street. I'd like to report a break-in. The criminal is still—"

"No! You can't do that to me, Patrick. Hang up the phone! They will take me to jail. I have an outstanding warrant for some speeding tickets. Please!" Courtney ran over and snatched the phone out of Patrick's hand.

Patrick grabbed Courtney's arm and spoke in a calm voice. "Give me back the phone, Court. And give me my key. Every single copy you made. The cops are still going to come. They have the address. It's only a matter of time. If you don't want me to give them your name when they get here, you'd better give me every key and promise not to pull any crap like this ever again."

Courtney went over to her purse, took out about five or six copies of the key and threw them at Patrick before grabbing her coat and fleeing from the apartment.

Before she left, she made a point of looking back at Aisha and glaring. "She's not better than me. But if you want to settle for less, fine. I'm tired of running after your ass!" With that, she slammed the door hard enough to break the thing off the hinges.

Aisha couldn't help herself. She started laughing. She was standing in the middle of Patrick's living room in her bra and panties and he was in his boxers with keys at his feet and one key stuck to his chest. And she thought it was the funniest thing that had ever happened to her. It was certainly the funniest altercation she'd ever seen.

"Man, she was a piece of work. What did you ever see in her? She's probably a class-A sociopath. She has delusions of grandeur… Hell, she's just delusional." Aisha plopped down on the love seat. She wasn't sitting on that sofa after the scantly clad insane chick had been all over it doing Lord knows what.

Patrick plucked the key off his chest, shook his head and dialed the phone again. "Hi, I'm calling from 750 East 30th Street and I'd like to cancel my previous call. It looked like a break-in, but it wasn't. Sorry for any inconvenience." He hung up the phone.

"I'm sorry you had to see that." He ran his hand over his head as he placed the phone back on the hook and picked up the keys, along with their clothing.

"Well, I said I didn't want to see a movie, but it looks like we got a little live drama anyway…some real live theater." Aisha stood up and walked over to him. "Your crazy ex-wife kind of ruined the mood. But we could—"

He stopped her words by pulling her into his arms and kissing her. Every nerve ending in her body bounced into awareness and she suddenly forgot all the nonsense she had been spouting about the mood being ruined.

When he finally stopped, she had a moment to catch her breath and try to slow down her heartbeat, which was pumping at a breakneck pace.

He lifted her up in his arms and carried her to his bedroom. When he placed her on the bed, he arched his eyebrow playfully. "You were saying?"

"Nothing." She opened her arms, reaching for him. "Nothing at all."

He climbed into the bed and picked up her left foot, massaging it with his hands and staring at her intently. He lifted the foot to his lips and kissed the tip of her big toe before sucking it deep in his mouth.

An electric shock spread from her foot, up her leg and right to her core. She moaned softly and felt as if her entire body were turning to jelly. The massage, the sucking—she didn't know which was more potent. She just knew she wanted more. When he repeated the action on her right foot, moaning could no longer suffice. She had to let out a good old-fashioned holler.

She took him in with her eyes, every ripple, every muscle. She wanted to touch him, but she could barely move.

"Is the mood still ruined for you, Aisha?" He let her foot go and began to tenderly knead her legs and thighs, trailing kisses as he went along.

She let out a hiss of breath and let her fingers brush his head, tangle with his hair, anything to keep her from placing her hands in her mouth and biting them off in order to deal with the ripples of pleasure he was causing.

And when he moved his way up to her core, she nearly wept. He opened her already slick folds and found her clitoris, ready, waiting, pulsing. His thumb touched her there. Once. Twice. And she was gone, shaking and coming undone. He barely waited for her to stop; instead, he began to lick and suck her into another frenzy.

"Mmm…that doesn't taste like the mood is ruined to me, love."

She had to scream then. She let out a howl that was so loud it made her wonder if his neighbors could hear her. And he went on about his business. Licking his way up her body until he reached her nipples. He massaged her breasts and suckled her nipples as if he had all the time in the world to pay homage to them.

She moaned over and over and over again. The sound had become one long, needful thing by the time he grabbed a condom and entered her.

There was no slow careful penetration this time. He entered her quickly, sharply, his own need finally taking hold of him. His thrusts were deep and strong. The fullness threatened to send her spiraling again and there was nothing she could do to stop it. He went in and out, over and over. And soon her eyes started to glaze over and she couldn't do anything but wrap her arms around him and cry out for joy. His lips, slowly, gingerly caressed hers as his hands gripped her bottom and he pulled her tightly to him. The soft kiss went in total contrast to the tight hold and deep, demanding thrusts. But it all felt so right, too right. They both screamed out their release and he held her in his arms. She never wanted him to let her go.

"Mood still ruined, love?"

She sighed. "If you have to ask after that, then maybe we need an encore."

He chuckled. "We have plenty of encores tonight, love. Plenty."

The next day, as they walked up to her apartment building after returning from the movies, Aisha noticed Bill and Dillon standing there. Bill was pacing in front of her building, looking as irritated and disgusted as he normally did and Dillon sat on the steps, looking forlorn and dejected.

The blood under her skin began to heat and bubble over as she began to think of all the reasons why her child would look like that. If Bill had put his hands on her baby, they might as well call the police now, because she was going to find a way to hurt him.

She dashed forward, leaving Patrick to follow as she dropped her leftover popcorn and placed her arms around Dillon. She checked his little brown face for any marks and studied him to see if he had been crying.

"Now your ass shows up! Where the hell have you been, Aisha? I did not take the boy so that you can whore around with your fireman." The ugliness in Bill's voice had a way of seeping into the air and sullying everything around him.

"You definitely want to watch how you speak to

Aisha in front of your son. But if you're as smart as you want people to think you are, you probably want to watch how you speak to her period." Patrick stood by her and Dillon with his arms folded across his chest. Patrick's stance was firm, unyielding and all male. But she had to search for the kind of anger and ugliness that normally went with that kind of show of testosterone. She only found the anger, a hint of it just at the surface, that was controlled and leashed but ready to pounce.

The differences between the two men were many. But the steady, calm control of Patrick Hightower showed her that he was a man she could trust.

"You don't tell me how to speak in front of my child or my wife," Bill snapped.

"Ex-wife." She and Patrick spoke the words in unison and watched as Bill's face turned an unsightly shade of red.

"Are you okay, sweetie?" She turned her attention to her son. "You're back a day early. Did something happen?" She could probably get more answers from Dillon anyway.

Dillon shrugged his little shoulders. "I'm fine. Can we just go upstairs now? I want to go home."

"The boy is fine. I have an emergency business meeting and I couldn't very well take him with me. And I'm running late as it is. If you're going to use the custody arrangement as some kind of chance for you to go out and slut about this godforsaken town, then perhaps I should see about full custody. I don't want all kinds of men around my son."

She felt the controlled anger in Patrick snap as soon as Bill said the word *slut* and she reached back to keep him from doing Bill bodily harm.

"Watch your mouth," Patrick said through clenched teeth before he turned to her. "Love, take Dillon upstairs. I'll be up in a second. I need to have a talk with your ex-husband."

She nodded, took her baby's hand and tried to swallow back her more-than-noticeable relief as she entered her apartment. As she looked down at Dillon, she could have sworn that she saw him grin. He certainly didn't look as forlorn as he had earlier. Maybe Patrick Hightower was exactly what they needed after all.

Patrick counted to ten, mainly because he would never hear the end of it if one of his brothers or cousins had to arrest him for assault and battery.

At least Bill had the sense to look a little frightened. *Chump.* Any man who would ever put his hands on a woman wasn't fit to breathe as far as Patrick was concerned. But he reminded himself that he wasn't judge and jury.

"You should know that I will press charges and sue you for everything you have if you so much as lay a hand on me." Bill started walking backward.

"And you should know that if you ever put your hands on Aisha or Dillon, or if I ever catch you saying those vile things about her again, you probably won't be able to press charges *or* sue." Patrick let his words sink in.

"Threats, Mr. Fireman?" Bill said snidely, all the while still moving toward his car.

"Promises, Billy-boy. You should know that I come from a family of cops and firemen. We protect and serve and have a code of honor that a lowlife like you could never even comprehend. On an ordinary day the thought of committing a crime would go against every fiber of our being. But if something or someone is threatening the people we love…then all bets are off." He gave Bill a heated glare. "You don't want to be the thing threatening the people I love. You just don't want that."

"They were my family first and I don't give up—"

"You gave up on your family the day you put your hands on her. And I'm telling you… You don't ever want to do something as foolish as that again. I can promise you that it wouldn't be a good idea health-wise."

Bill made it to the curb where his car was parked and nearly tripped over himself trying to get into the little sports car and glare at Patrick at the same time.

Patrick shook his head. He didn't trust the fool. But he hoped the man was smarter than he looked, because he would seriously hurt him if he ever hurt Aisha or Dillon.

After Aisha and Dillon finished their pizza dinner, she decided to curl up with one of her romance novels while she let Dillon watch one of his action cartoon DVDs. Just when she was getting to one of the good parts there was a knock on the door.

Her heart stopped for a moment because she thought

it could have been Bill coming back. She knew she had pushed it by being so "mouthy," the phrase he'd used whenever she stood up for herself when they were married. She'd tried to be brave and stand up to him, but it was hard to do so when she remembered just how cruel he could be. And if he was coming back for another round, she worried that she wouldn't be able to finish this one unscathed.

She took a calming breath and walked down the hall to the door. At least her child was trained properly and knew not to open the door unless she told him.

When she peered through the peephole she was more surprised by what she saw.

Sandra Clemmons-Foster. Her mother.

If she were a superstitious woman she would have thought it was some kind of omen. First her father called, then Bill showed up and now her mother was at her doorstep. She'd spent the past five years hardly ever hearing from them, and now she couldn't seem to shake them. Her father and Bill must really have wanted Bill to be promoted to partner if her dad had actually let her mother come visit her.

She opened the door. "Hi, Mom." She stepped aside to let in the woman who had raised, nurtured and loved her while she was growing up.

Her mother stepped in, and as soon as her eyes fell on Dillon they lit up. Aisha found it hard to believe that her mother hadn't actually seen her grandson in person in five years. Aisha sent her a copy of Dillon's school pictures each year, but nothing made up for face time.

"Dillon, come give your grandmother a hug. You remember your grandmother, don't you?" Aisha motioned for her son to come over to them.

Dillon walked over and cautiously embraced Sandra. The glee in her mother's smile warmed Aisha's heart.

Sandra ruffled Dillon's curls and squeezed him tightly before reluctantly letting him go.

Her mother looked thinner than her normal shapely self and it gave Aisha some concern. Sandra had cut her usually long salt-and-pepper-streaked hair into a bouncy shoulder-length bob.

"Hi, Grandma." Once free, Dillon took off to catch the rest of his DVD.

"Hi, baby." Sandra's hand went out as if she wanted to get another touch of Dillon.

"Dillon, baby, can you go back in your bedroom for a little bit while I talk to Grandma in the living room?"

"Aww…Mom…it's just getting to the good part…" Dillon whined.

"Let him watch his show. We can talk in the kitchen. I can't stay long anyway. I need to be back in Montclair well before your father gets back from his lodge meetings." Sandra made scare quotes in the air as she said the word *lodge* and let Aisha know that she was under no illusions about where her husband spent his once-a-week outings.

Aisha had always suspected that her father was having a long-standing affair. But since he actually belonged to a lodge and they did meet once a week, she could never really be sure.

"Well, okay." Since this was the first time her mother had graced her apartment, she wanted to at least entertain her in the living room, but the kitchen would have to do.

"Would you like some tea or water or something, Mom?"

"No, sit down. Don't put yourself out for me. Like I said, I can't really stay long. I just wanted to come here and see you. I wanted to make sure that you weren't considering going to back to him." Sandra placed her hand over Aisha's across the table.

"Going back to who? Bill? No way. You don't have to worry about that."

Sandra let out a breath of relief and her eyes fluttered. "I know I haven't been the best example all these years. But you're out and you're doing okay. And you seem happy, Aisha…. I know how your father can get when he wants his way. But you didn't let them break you. So don't go back. Okay?" She squeezed Aisha's hand.

Aisha's heart felt as if it was in her throat. She knew the risk her mother had taken coming there. "Mom, you know you don't have to stay, either. You can leave."

Sandra gave a lighthearted laugh that sounded like anything but. "No. It's too late for me. I'm too set in my ways and I'm not nearly as brave as you. I couldn't have done what you did. But you did it *in spite of* me and how I raised you. I raised you to be quiet and meek and not to stand up for yourself, because I was so scared. But you overcame everything, and I'm proud of you."

"I'm still afraid, Mom, of so many things. But none

of that is your fault. I'm an adult. I have to take responsibility for my on life and my own choices."

Sandra sighed. "Your father was ranting and raving about you seeing some fireman. Is that true? Does he make you happy?"

Aisha closed her eyes, remembering the fib she had told her father. She didn't want to lie to her mother. And she certainly didn't want to spend what little time they had together talking about a relationship that probably wouldn't happen, probably wouldn't happen because she was too scared to try….

"Mom, if you wanted to you could leave, too. You don't have to stay. I know my place is small, but you're more than welcome here."

"No. I made my bed." She paused. "You know, your father wasn't always so…the way he is… I mean… He was always controlling, and hard, but not so…so… mean…. I think I've been a disappointment to him ever since I couldn't give him a son—"

"It wasn't your fault you kept miscarrying, Mom. Don't blame yourself for that." Aisha knew that her father had always wanted a son, and that he saw Bill as the son he'd never had. But she refused to let her mother take the blame for her father's issues, and she certainly wasn't going to take the blame because she divorced the man who was like a son to him.

"How can I not when he just got meaner and meaner with each child we lost? It was something he couldn't control and he doesn't like it when he can't control things. That's why you have to stay free and be happy, even if it means we won't be able to see one another. If you give in to your father and William it won't make your father happy. *Nothing* you do will make him happy. I made my bed, but you got away. I really hope that fireman is more worthy of your love than William was. I want you to be happy, Aisha. Will you be happy for me?" Sandra got up and gave Aisha's hand one more squeeze.

Aisha smiled and tried to hold back the tears threatening to spill from her eyes as she pulled her mother into an embrace. It was such a small request really. And she wondered if she could gather the braveness her mother seemed to think she had and actually do what her mother wanted her to do. Could she break past all her barriers and go after her own happiness? Was she brave enough to try love again?

After saying goodbye to her mother and putting her son to bed, Aisha reflected on the bad choices she had made when she was thinking about her father's happiness and not her own. She thought about everything that had gone into her decision to marry Bill. And then she thought about Patrick and she smiled.

Chapter 11

If she had any second thoughts about spending Thanksgiving with Patrick and his family, it was too late now. They had been going pretty hot and heavy for over three months and things were running smoothly between them. But was it really time to meet his family?

They pulled up to the family's Tudor-style mini-mansion.

"Your home is lovely," Aisha said to Patrick's parents.

Dillon handed Celia Hightower the fall flowers that they had brought for her.

"Why thank you so much, young man. Aren't you just precious—and handsome, too? I love getting flowers from handsome young men." Celia Hightower winked at her husband and then handed him the flowers.

"Here, honey, place these in a vase and put them right on the dining-room table for everyone to see.

"Thank you for the compliment, Aisha. We're so glad you and Dillon could join us. I've heard so much about the two of you." Celia Hightower gave Dillon a hug and then gave Aisha one.

"Patrick, why don't you get them introduced to everyone. I'm finishing up things in the kitchen. Well…sort of, my new daughter-in-law, Minerva, is a whiz in the kitchen and she has thankfully taken over with the help of my other daughters-in-law, Samantha and Penny. I'm just happy I don't have to do all the cooking for this gang all alone anymore." Celia paused and turned to Aisha. "Do you want to come in the kitchen and help us?"

Dillon cleared his little throat and then he and Patrick had the nerve to bust out laughing.

Traitors!

Oh, well, might as well come clean… "I love the idea of cooking and I experiment with recipes a lot, Mrs. Hightower. But I'm not that great at it." Aisha reached out and pulled both Dillon's and Patrick's ears and twisted them before letting go.

That'll teach them to make fun of my culinary creations in front of new people again.

Mrs. Hightower laughed and pulled Aisha along. "Please, call me Celia. Then you can just relax and watch right along with me. And if I were you, I wouldn't cook a thing for those two for at least a month. We'll see who'll be laughing then."

"Cool!" Dillon pumped his little fist.

She was going to have to have a talk with her little man about tact and decorum. And given the way Patrick was laughing and patting her son on the back, she was going to have to have a talk with her big man, too.

"Girl, don't even study them. My first year of marriage, I burned everything I cooked. And you'd better believe that James Hightower grinned and ate it."

Aisha laughed. "Dillon will grin and make jokes, but he won't eat it if it doesn't taste good."

They entered the kitchen and Aisha's mouth fell open. Since she'd became addicted to the Food Network and had started to fantasize about preparing fabulous meals in her dream kitchen, she had a pretty good idea of what that looked like. And the Hightowers certainly had a dream kitchen.

Everything from the stainless-steel appliances to the marble countertops and cherrywood cabinets and furnishings had her standing there with her mouth wide-open. The creations and concoctions she could make in a kitchen like this! She was willing to bet money that the recipes would come out perfectly every time if she had a kitchen like this one. How could they not?

"Hey, girlfriend!" Samantha came over and gave Aisha a big hug.

Minerva placed a pie in the oven before coming over and embracing Aisha. "Y'all, this is the woman we said might be the one who stole Patrick's heart."

Aisha found herself blushing.

Another woman with long sisterlocks and pretty

copper eyes got up from the kitchen table where she was playing with a little girl who looked just like her. She lifted the toddler to her hip and walked over to them.

"Hi, my name is Penny, and I'm married to Jason, Patrick's youngest brother. It's great to meet you."

Celia took her grandbaby out of Penny's arms.

"Gramma." The little girl placed her chubby little hands on Celia's face and slobbered on the woman's check.

"Say hi to Ms. Aisha, Cee Cee," Celia said as she took Cee Cee's little hand and waved it for the toddler. "Aisha, this is my grandbaby, Celia Carla Hightower. We call her Cee Cee."

"Hi there, Cee Cee. Aren't you the most beautiful little girl in the world?" Aisha waved at the little handful.

"Hi, Miss I-sha." Cee Cee did her best to mimic the words her grandmother had said and waved back at Aisha.

"Hey, everybody, where the food at?" A petite and curvy light-skinned woman came prancing into the kitchen and walked right over to Celia and Cee Cee. "Hey, look at my little mini-me. How's granny's little sweet meat? How's my baby girl?" The woman took Cee Cee from Celia's arms and shooed Celia away. "I got her. Y'all need to do the damn thang and get this show on the road. A chick is hungry up in this piece."

Aisha noticed Penny roll her eyes and shake her head.

"Mama, give me Cee Cee and go on and sit down somewhere. Unless you want to help with the preparations," Penny said.

"I'll help by holding mini-me while y'all do the damn thang and cook. Right, mini-me?"

Cee Cee grabbed hold of the woman's face and slobbered a kiss on her cheek.

"Look at you giving granny all your sugar. That's granny's little sweet meat." The woman looked at Aisha, and then she turned to the other women in the room. "Harpo, who dis woman?" She then burst out laughing at her own joke.

Aisha squinted her eyes and turned to the other women in the room. Was this woman for real? She didn't think she had ever met anyone like her before. In fact, she was pretty sure she hadn't.

"Hi, my name is Aisha. I came with Patrick."

The women reared back with a gut-busting laugh and little Cee Cee held on for the ride, giggling and laughing with her granny. Aisha wondered if anyone else was at all worried about the child's safety in the arms of a slightly touched woman.

"Get out of here! Patrick found somebody to put up with his ol' cranky self? Well, ain't that a blip? My name is Carla, and I'm Penny's mom and the cutest little girl in the world's granny."

"All right, ladies, we can start bringing platters into the dining room. Soup's on." Minerva headed out with the green bean casserole.

Aisha figured she couldn't mess up carrying the platters, so she chipped in and helped bring things out.

Once the buffet table was all set up, folks started coming in, fixing their plates and taking seats at the table.

Since she had been an only child, she had never experienced this kind of large family gathering. It was a nice feeling. It felt like something out of one of those movies, *Soul Food* or *This Christmas* or something like that. She decided she liked it a lot and could get used to it.

The doorbell rang as the last of their bunch were serving themselves and Aisha could hardly believe her eyes.

Who in the hell invited Patrick's crazy ex-wife? Another woman with a severely tight bun on the top of her head walked in behind *Crazy Courtney,* the name Aisha had become fond of calling Patrick's ex.

"Hello, everyone, I hope y'all don't mind that I brought a guest. Courtney is back in town and since she is still just like family, I thought it would be great to invite her to Thanksgiving." The tight-bun lady made the statement as if she ran the household and was daring anyone to have a problem with it.

Aisha made a point of checking out each and every face in the room. They all looked shocked and appalled.

The only person who didn't appear shocked was Penny's mother, Carla. She simply broke out into a wide grin that showed her front chipped tooth in all its grandeur and shook her head.

"Who in the hell left the gate open? That's all I wanna know right now. Ha!" Carla laughed even harder, even though she was the only one laughing.

Courtney looked around the table with a big fake phony smile on her face. "Hi, everybody." She chirped in her overly bright, overly happy, overly overly everything voice. When she saw Aisha, her smile froze and dropped. "What the hell is *she* doing here? Patrick, what is she doing here? I know I saw y'all together, but damn. I'm part of this family, not this little trick."

"Harpo, who dis woman?" Carla tried her joke once again and this time at least one of Patrick's brothers laughed.

Aisha didn't know for sure which one of Patrick's brothers was cracking up, but since he was sitting by Samantha and Samantha herself seemed as if she could barely contain her laughter, Aisha assumed that the laughing brother was Joel.

Aisha would have laughed, too, if she wasn't trying to keep her wits about her. Because if something jumped off, she was protecting her child first and taking off Courtney's head—lace-front wig and all.

Patrick glared at Courtney first and then at the older woman. "It's none of your business why she's here, Courtney. She was invited. You were not."

"I was too invited—by your aunt." Courtney glowered, turned and poked the older woman. "You said he wasn't serious about her or you would know. You said I had a chance."

"Sophie, what kind of mess are you bringing into my home?" James Hightower spoke in a low but powerful voice.

"This is so-o-o not worth it! I should have stayed in Trenton. Sophie, if you think I'm the only one going out like a sucker, you're wrong! I'm taking your high and mighty behind with me." Courtney's face took on an evil glare. "Sophie can't stand the thought of Celia in this home and she wants me and Patrick to get back together and have a family so that you will be forced to give the house to your oldest living son and his family. She figures she can move in once me and Patrick get back together. But the way she has been messing things up, I'm not so sure if I'd like that now. This has been very traumatic for me." Courtney placed her hand over her head and plopped down in a seat.

Aisha noticed that she did it carefully, so as not to disturb the lace-front wig.

"Courtney, you need to leave. And Sophie, so do you." Celia Hightower stood up and walked over to the women. "A house, Sophie? You have been acting like this all these years over a damn house? Do you know you can have this damn house?"

"Awwww sookie sookie now! It's about to be on up in here. I ain't never seen my girl Celia get this angry. She's usually the calm one. Go head, Celia, let the Fourth Ward come out of you, girl. I knew it was in there. Rep yo hood!" Carla leaned forward as if she didn't want to miss a thing. "I told you it was going to be some mess we wouldn't want to miss. And you didn't want to come, Gerald. If I had missed this, mannnnnn!" Carla elbowed the man sitting next to her and he did his best to ignore her.

Aisha could only assume that he was Penny's father, since he had the same copper-colored eyes.

"Mommy!" Penny snapped.

"What?" Carla snapped back. "I'm just saying if

stuff jumps off in here, I got yo back, Celia. It's about to be on up in here and I'm ready. I've been waiting a long time for this."

Courtney's eyes widened when she looked at Carla, and Aisha didn't blame her. The small woman looked like she could kick butts and take names all day long.

"I don't want to fight anyone…." Courtney started looking around the table and backing away.

"Then you'd best leave," Celia said in the same low, hard and angry voice she'd been using since Sophie and Courtney arrived. "Anybody who has been told to leave my house had better leave if they don't want to be hurt."

This time Sophie started backing up, too.

"You can't ride with me, Sophie. I'm through with you filling my head up with nonsense. I had a good thing going in Trenton and ruined it with this bull." Courtney glared at Aisha and Patrick before leaving. "He ain't hardly worth all this drama anyway." Courtney made a production of stomping out of the dining room and soon they heard the front door slam.

Sophie tried to move away from Celia, but Celia had latched onto her arm.

"James, can you take me home now?"

"I didn't bring you here, Sophie. And I told you if you couldn't come here and act civil then you shouldn't have come. You came here knowing you were going to be starting this mess." James made motions as if he were washing his hands of his sister.

"Come with me, Sophie. Let me talk to you for a

minute." Celia started walking off and pulling Sophie along with her.

"Not if you're going to hit me again," Sophie screeched and tried to drag her feet. "James, please! Your wife has obviously lost her mind. Patrick! Lawrence! Jason! Joel! Please."

Nobody made a move to help the woman as Celia dragged her away.

"Whew! Now that was some drama! And y'all High-towers think our family has drama. I'll tell you, I get my fill of drama when I come over here. You watch, new girl…whatever you name is… Mark my words—they have some drama up in this piece every time Sophie brings her old crusty hateful behind around."

"Carla, hush!" Gerald seemed a little embarrassed by his wife's running mouth.

"What? Ain't no shame in my game. That ain't even how I roll. And as much drama as they got going, it ought not be no shame in they game, either."

Patrick cleared his throat. "I apologize for any drama brought on by my ex-wife. I don't know what Aunt Sophie has been filling her head with, but she needs to stop it."

"And what is this about Aunt Sophie being scared that Mama is going to hit her? Mama wouldn't hurt a fly," Jason piped in.

"Mama used to be in a gang, so she might just give Sophie something to be afraid of after all these years," Lawrence offered. "And I'm going on record now, letting y'all know that if Mama does bring it to Sophie, I. Am. Not. Arresting. My. Mama!"

"I'm not arresting Mama, either," Jason added.

"Nobody's arresting my wife!" James looked at them all so that they were all clear. "It'll be fine. Just eat your food and change the subject."

Dillon glanced up at Aisha and she shrugged at him. She had been an only child and so was her son. Neither one of them had had any experience with this kind of large-family dynamics. But she certainly found it entertaining.

"A house, Sophie? You have treated me like crap all these years because you didn't want me in this house? Do you really want to know what you can do with this house?" Celia couldn't believe her sister-in-law and former friend.

Sophie sat down on the bed. Tired and a little bit worn. "It wasn't just the house... It was more than the house."

She had made her sister-in-law come upstairs with her to one of the boys' old bedrooms that she had turned into a guest bedroom and sewing room. If they were going to have it out once and for all, she didn't want any interruptions this time.

"What was it then?" She sat down on the sewing bench in front of the bed, waiting for Sophie's answer and feeling a little tired herself.

Sophie paused and for a minute it seemed as if she wasn't going to say anything. Finally, she sighed, opened her mouth and closed it again.

"All of the sudden you have nothing to say? All these years you wouldn't shut up and now you're silent?"

Sophie glared at her. "First it was my mother thinking you weren't good enough and she convinced me that you had used me to nab my brother. And for years I held on to that, even after Mom died. And then you moved into this house and it became about the house and more. It was about you being too happy, and me being miserable. It was about you having a wonderful, handsome family and me having nothing. It was about all of that. And now, now I don't know what it is about."

"Do you hate me?" Celia folded her arms across her chest and waited for the answer.

"I don't hate you. But I'm sure you hate me after all this… All these years…"

"I never hated you, Sophie. I always thought that, one day, we would even be friends again. I thought, 'Once she sees how happy James is, how happy the boys are, how fine they grew up…' I've wasted all these years, allowed you to basically wreak havoc in my life because I wanted you to like me again. I wanted you to see me as worthy of your brother's love." A tear fell from her eye as she allowed herself to finally mourn the friendship she had lost with Sophie.

Celia wiped the tear away angrily. Too much had happened, too much hurt had been down for her to cry. Sophie didn't deserve her tears now. She straightened herself up and composed herself. Sophie's bringing Courtney back into Patrick's life for a house was the last straw.

"Courtney was a vile, selfish woman who nearly

broke my son's heart. He's luckily found a woman who allows him to experience joy again. She's a nice woman, a schoolteacher—"

"That woman has a child. How could you want him to step into a ready-made family? He deserves better than that." Sophie gave a bitter laugh and that was when Celia knew there was no hope for the woman.

If she couldn't see that beautiful little boy as a benefit, as an added bonus to any relationship, then she was just hopeless.

"He deserves a woman who loves him enough not to cheat on him. He deserves love. And he's found it. If I hear that you have been up to your tricks trying to break them up the way you did with Jason and Joel and Lawrence…I will beat your ass." Celia stood there and let her words sink in.

"I'm going to call you a cab. I don't know what happened to you. What happened to my friend and mentor? I don't know why you became so bitter and miserable. But I can't allow you to hurt me or the ones I love—"

"I would never hurt any of your children. I love them. They are a part of my brother and a part of you…" Sophie's voice trailed off. "I poured every ounce of love I had into my nephews. You have to know that, Celia."

"Yes, I know that, Sophie. I know you love my sons. And I know that you love your brother. But you have to learn to love people without conditions, even when they love people you don't." Celia got up from the bench and walked toward the door. "I hope one day you realize that we all love you. You were my friend, Sophie."

Celia walked out of the room feeling several pounds lighter, as if a weight had been lifted off her chest. She no longer held out hope that she and her sister-in-law would regain their closeness. But she also no longer carried the burden of their failed friendship. That burden was Sophie's now.

Sophie rode home in the cab feeling as if the weight of the world had been placed on her shoulders. Nothing had gone as planned and that insipid Courtney had caused her to lose everything.

She had truly lost everything—everything and everyone that ever really mattered to her. She doubted that Patrick would have any time for her anymore. He hadn't even told her about his new love interest. A schoolteacher, just like Celia. It was funny that all four boys had found women who, each in her own way, shared similarities with Celia. Her Celia…

What would Celia have said if Sophie had told her the truth? That all those years ago, she had been jealous because Celia chose James over their friendship. She could never have acted on what she felt for Celia, not back then, and certainly not now… She hadn't lied when she said that she didn't hate Celia.

She had never hated Celia.

She probably never would.

Celia did know that Sophie could no longer be

Celia's friend. If Sophie had tried to continue to be Celia's friend after she picked her brother over their friendship, she would have been even more miserable than she had been all these years. She knew that with certainty.

She had made peace with the Lord many years ago when she decided that she wouldn't act on her desires. But she had never made peace with herself. And for that reason, happiness was never destined to be hers.

Chapter 12

Patrick couldn't believe that he had finally found *the one*. He certainly never knew or believed that a woman like Aisha Miller could have possibly existed. Just being around her soothed all the cold and hardened parts of his life. And he was so in love with her son that he couldn't wait until the day when he could make it official and become a real father to the young boy.

The only problem was that Patrick wasn't sure if Aisha felt the same way he did. He was willing to lay it all on the line and stick around to find out, though. After months of getting to know her and her son, he had fallen madly in love with both mother and child.

He had a special lineup planned for her Valentine's Day weekend that he hoped she would enjoy. She was spending the weekend at his place. The first night he would wow her by preparing a fancy dinner, and on Saturday night—Valentine's Day—he was going to take her out for dinner and dancing at a fancy nuevo soul supper club. It was going to be a group outing with his brothers and their wives.

Luckily for him, he prepared meals all the time at the fire station. But this meal was special. It was his first weekend off in a while and he wanted to make it extraordinary for Aisha. She had been holding up rather well, letting Dillon go with his father for the weekends. And Patrick knew it was extremely difficult when he had to work or when she didn't have the book club to keep her busy. But she kept an upbeat attitude and she had at least stopped talking about taking Dillon and moving away.

"It smells wonderful in here." Aisha sniffed the air and pouted. "If I weren't about to enjoy this wonderful meal, I would be jealous of you in here cooking like this."

"Don't be jealous, love. As Dillon says, you make the best baked chicken and rice in the world." He chuckled when he noticed her eyes narrow. "Here, taste this." He held the wooden spoon, filled with sauce from his chicken Marsala, to her lips and she sipped.

"Mmm… You are awesome. That was so-oo good. I'm starving. Feed me. Feed me."

"Patience, love, patience."

"You need any help? I can do something or make something. I can do the salad."

"Okay…the veggies and stuff are in the crisper and—"

"Cool! I've been dying to try this thing I saw Pat and Gina do with a salad on 'Down Home with the Neelys'—"

"You know what? This is my treat for you and we can't have you in here working when it's supposed to be my treat to you now, can we? How about you go and pick out some music instead?"

She stopped by the refrigerator door and frowned. "But I want to help you."

"I know, and you can help by relaxing, turning on some music, having a glass of wine and letting me spoil you this evening."

"Mmm-hmm… How about if I just made a plain old boring salad and didn't try to create anything I'd seen on TV? Would you want me to help then?"

"If that's possible for you to do. If you can take out and use only the ingredients I have set aside for the salad, then yes, I'd love for you to help me."

"Fine, I'll make your old boring salad."

"Lettuce, tomatoes, cucumbers, red onion, croutons and Italian dressing. It's all in the fridge."

"Mmm-hmm…" She opened the fridge and took out the ingredients. She washed them and sliced and diced them into a perfect salad.

"Now wasn't that easy?" He teased.

"Too, easy… Hey how about I boil up some eg—"

"Nah, that's fine."

She poked out her lips and scrunched up her eyes for a minute before brightening. "That bottle dressing is so pedestrian. If you have some EVOO and some mustard and some vinegar, either red wine vinegar or apple cider, although I'm sure I could improvise and use regular vinegar. I don't see why not." She got up and started looking through the cabinets.

"Um... EVOO? What's that? And more important, what're you doing?"

"I'm going to make a wonderful homemade salad dressing for your regular, plain, boring salad. EVOO is what Rachael Ray calls extra virgin olive oil. Cute, huh?"

"Yeah, cute, but unfortunately, we don't have time for a homemade dressing today. Dinner is ready and I can't wait for you to taste it. So just have a seat and I will serve you, my sweet."

"Oooo... I like that. Okay, but next time, I'm cooking for you. I've got a bunch of new recipes I want to try out."

"And I can't wait to try them. But tonight, it's all about me serving you. So go sit down." He gave her a gentle pat on the behind and she giggled.

Once the food was served and they were both seated, he poured her a glass of sauvignon blanc and then poured himself a glass. He held up his glass for a toast and she followed.

"To us."

"To us," she repeated.

"So, tell me, love, what is it about trying new things in the kitchen that moves you so much? You're a good cook."

"Yeah, yeah, I make the best baked chicken and rice... Boring..."

"Have you thought of maybe not improvising with

the new recipes until you've been cooking them for a while first? Or maybe you can improvise with the so-called boring dishes you already make well…throw a different seasoning on the baked chicken, you know?"

She shot him a look and twisted up her lips. "I suppose." She took a bite of her food. "This is really good. The chicken is so tender and juicy. And the sauce… Mmm… This sauce is to die for. I think I officially can't stand you now. Where did you learn to cook like this?"

"The firehouse. We are each responsible for meals on different days and where most of the guys would have their wives make something and bring it in, as a single guy, I had to prepare my own dishes. And ordering out for that bunch would have burned a hole in my pocket after a while."

She nodded and then she got a devilish look on her face. "So have you had any more scantily clad women breaking into your home lately? Whatever happened to Crazy Courtney? We haven't heard from her in a while."

"Thank goodness! I went to visit Aunt Sophie the other day and she said that Courtney hightailed it back to Trenton and is no longer talking to her."

"How's your aunt?"

"She's fine. She was surprised to see that I still stopped by to see her. I think my brother, Jason, my dad and I are the only ones who do. But as crazy as she is, she is still my aunt. She's always tried to look out for me. Plus, she knows better than to try and do anything to mess up my relationship with you. I think Aunt Sophie has finally calmed down."

"I don't know if I'd count her out yet. From what I heard from Minerva and Samantha at the book club, Aunt Sophie is a mess. She gave Penny and Samantha hell. And she tried to give Minerva hell, too."

Patrick laughed. "Minerva is a tough cookie. She has to be to put up with Lawrence."

"Your brother is a big ol' softie, just like you."

"Don't let him hear you say that. He has a reputation to uphold. And so do I. I'm gruff and grumpy Patrick."

"With a smile like that? I don't think so. And I know Cee Cee, Dillon, Joel Jr. and Jason Jr. would disagree. No, let's face it, you're a big ol' teddy bear."

He winced before chuckling. "Speaking of my partner in crime, how's Dillon adjusting to his weekend visits with his dad? How are you adjusting?"

"I think we're both adjusting as well as we can. I'll tell you what made me feel a little better about it is today before he came for Dillon, I was having a hard time getting Dillon to get ready. And Dillon said his dad hardly spent time with him anyway. He spent most of his time with Grandmother and Grandfather."

Disgusted, he snapped, "So he's pawning Dillon off on his parents?"

"No, *my* parents! Can you believe that? My mother can't call me or come see her grandson at my house because her husband, my father, forbids it. But she can babysit her grandson during the weekend for her trifling, abusive, low-life ex-son-in-law. Does that make any sense to you?"

Patrick had to lean back and scratch his head on that one. He couldn't imagine anyone being able to keep his mother away from her grandbabies. Also, the thought of Bill taking Dillon away from his loving mother over the weekends only to leave him in someone else's care both baffled and angered Patrick. He couldn't understand it. If he were lucky enough to have a son like Dillon one day, he'd gladly spend every moment he could with the kid.

"The man is an idiot. And, sorry to say it, but your parents are idiots, too."

But their loss is my gain, because I don't ever intend to let you go.

"Yes. I know. The thing is, even though I'm glad my mom is getting to spend time with Dillon, and I know she really wants to, she's too afraid of my dad to just come to my house and see her grandson. I don't want Dillon picking up any bad habits from them, either. My dad can be really harsh and some of the things he says to my mom… The way he speaks to her…his tone…" She shuddered.

"Dillon will know better, Aisha. We'll teach him better."

"We?"

"That's right—*we*. I'm in it for the long haul, love. You just try getting rid of me."

She broke out laughing and took a sip of her wine. "Oh, I gave up trying to do that a week after I met you. It became very clear to me that you had no intention of going away. So I figured I'd let you hang around."

"That's right, smart girl. I like my women smart." He got up and started clearing off the table.

"And you came in handy, too. Just look at this delicious meal you prepared." She got up to help him.

They worked together to clean up the kitchen and put away the dishes. Then he poured them each another glass of wine and led her into the living room. He turned on the CD player and Luther's "Take You Out" filled the room. He took their glasses, placed them on coasters and pulled her into his arms.

"You know this is my theme song. You had a man begging for a date for a long time before you said yes. I felt like Luther…" He sang along with the lyrics. "Can I take you out tonight?"

She grinned and swayed with him to the mellow beat and Luther's soulful crooning. "I didn't make you beg that long. And all those outings we went on with Dillon felt a lot like dates to me."

"A brother had to do what a brother had to do. I had to take any opening I could, because I couldn't let you get away."

"Aw… That's the cutest reason for stalking and using a woman's kid to get at her soft spot I ever heard." She laughed when he frowned.

"I'm not a stalker. That's my brother, Lawrence." He spun her around.

"I'm going to tell him you said that when we see him tomorrow."

He gave her another whirl. "Tell him. I tell him that

all the time." He chuckled and pulled her close when another of Luther's greatest hits came on.

"I love how close your family is, how tight that family bond is…. Everyone is just so nice and so close. I'm glad Dillon is seeing this. I wouldn't mind at all if he grew up to be the kind of man you and your brothers are."

His heart became so full he almost stopped moving. Hearing those heartfelt words from her almost did him in. It almost made him tell her how much he loved her and never wanted to let her go. It made him want to tell her that he would be proud to be a role model for her son; that he wanted to be a second father to her son if she'd let him. But she wasn't ready to hear any of that. Even though he had made more progress with her in the past few months than he ever could have imagined, there was no way she was on the same page as he was.

"Dillon is a great kid and I know he's going to grow up to be a fine and upstanding man." *I'm going to make sure that he and the rest of our children are all the best people they can be, love.* Since he couldn't tell her what he was feeling, he figured he would show her.

He swooped down, captured her lips in a kiss and poured all the love his heart was feeling into it.

Aisha swore that she had never been kissed like this before—ever. Every time he kissed her he almost made her believe that he was really hers forever, but this time she did believe it. The kiss gave every single doubt in her mind a run for its money.

His tongue moved forward as if it were on a mission. It cased the perimeters of her mouth with deliberate and decided probing. He flicked the roof of her mouth, caressed her inner cheeks and trailed her teeth. He seemed to be getting to know every part of her mouth and she was more than willing to let him.

His hands tightened around her bottom, squeezing and pulling her forward. The closer she got to him, the more she could feel his heated arousal for her. She moaned because the memories of each mating they had shared were just *that good* and the anticipation of what was to come was just *that unbearable.*

They moved together to the music for a while, tongues and bodies tangled in a heated connection that neither wanted to break. It was only when their desire had sizzled over to the point of almost short-circuiting and exploding that he broke the kiss and slowly, methodically begin to undress her. He removed her cream sweater set first, leaving the pearls and her red lace bra.

She stepped out of her brown pumps, unbuttoned her pants and let them puddle on the floor. He watched her as he, too, removed his clothing.

She stood in her bra and thong and watched the mahogany god that appeared when he took off his clothing. Each muscle on his body was so well designed, so well placed, she thought he must have been a work of art. She reached out her hand and let it glide down his chest. The man could have been one of those Chippendale dancers. His body was that rock solid. His erection was standing at attention, covered in prophylactic, bold, strong, ready and waiting.

She licked her lips. "You're beautiful, Patrick. Absolutely gorgeous."

He pulled her close and she felt her nipples pebble when they brushed against his granite chest. He unsnapped her bra and walked her over to the love seat, bending her over as he went. When he reached the love seat, he gently spread her legs, leaned her over the side and entered her. The strength of his stroke had her grabbing the cushions and holding on for the ride.

He leaned into his thrust, clearly trying to reach depths he hadn't reached before. And she pushed back into him, wanting him to feel every single part of her. For some reason the Luther Vandross song that he jokingly said was his theme song came on again and the words made her heart burst.

As he moved in and out of her, she heard Luther singing, "I wanna know you, I think I could show you good love…" and tears fell from her eyes.

She couldn't for the life of her figure out why she'd had such a hard time giving him a chance when he'd been so up-front and so sincere from day one.

They moved together, soon making music all their own, the background music altogether forgotten.

He leaned forward and whispered in her ear. "You're the beautiful one, love. From the moment I saw you I knew you were the most beautiful woman I'd ever seen and the woman that I would judge every other woman against for the rest of my life. You are the one for me, Aisha. The only one."

He nipped her ear, causing a sharp jolt to run down her spine to her core. His hips did a deep piston, pressing her farther into the sofa. Each thrust made her pelvis rub against the leather, adding to the friction he caused inside her until she found herself screaming out at the top of her lungs. She felt herself tighten around him, so tight she didn't think she would ever come undone. But then he sped up and pushed her even further to her limit and she experienced a release more powerful than anything she had ever felt before.

He kept moving in and out, over and over, until he, too, found release with a deep-from-the-gut grunt and groan that seemed to speak to something deep inside her.

Her heart throbbed out of control and just like that she went from the rigid throes of orgasm to an almost Jell-O–like existence where she was thankful for the sofa in front of her. Without it, she knew she would have flopped on the ground.

Aisha couldn't move. So she figured she'd just hang out there until she could feel her legs again.

Then Patrick picked her up and swooped her into his arms. He planted a kiss on her forehead as he carried her back into the bedroom. She wrapped her arms around his neck and snuggled her head into his chest. The deep, woodsy, masculine smell of him made her want him all the more.

"You ready for round two, love?"

Round two? Oh. My. God.

She looked up at him questioningly as he placed her on the bed. "I'm ready if you are…"

"I'm more than ready, love. It's all about serving you this weekend." He then eased down her body and parted her thighs, readying her for the most intimate of kisses.

She tried to calm her shaking thighs and prepped herself for the second round of loving. But there was no way she could prepare herself for the orgasm that rocked through her as he spread apart her already love-slick folds and pressed against her already overly stimulated clitoris.

She screamed and took the ride, knowing that it would most certainly be worth it in the end.

Chapter 13

Aisha looked in the full-length mirror and could hardly believe her eyes. The little red dress she had picked up for their Valentine's Day evening looked amazing on her. She had been a little leery about buying it. But Toni went with her to look for something to wear and she had let the wild child talk her into buying something she normally wouldn't have even considered.

She was a sweater-set-and-pearls kind of a girl at heart. But tonight…tonight she was a diva! The low-cut, red-and-white-sequined bodice of the dress fit her form perfectly. The skirt stopped just a few inches shy of her knees, showing plenty of leg. The red-satin strappy stilettos she wore set everything off nicely. Now all she needed was someone to zip her up in the back and they could be on their way.

As if summoned by thought, Patrick came into his bedroom at that very moment. "You ready—" he started and paused. "We're going to be late."

"No, we aren't, silly. All I need you to do is zip me up and we'll be on our way." She reached behind her and wiggled to point out the zipper.

She glanced at him through the mirror and noticed him standing there, staring at her with his mouth open and his eyes hooded. She turned around then. "What's wrong with you? Come on and zip me up."

He walked forward, slowly, deliberately and looking like he was on the prowl. "We're going to be late," he repeated. "You're looking too damn good in that dress. And if you want it taken off without it being ruined, you should probably go ahead and take it off yourself."

He took off his suit jacket, laid it on the bed and started unbuttoning his shirt as he walked toward her.

She took a few steps back. "Are you serious? We made love all night last night and all morning and afternoon!"

"Do I look like I'm playing?" He took off his shirt and undershirt and she got a good look at his rippled chest. "The dress, love… I don't trust myself not to ruin it, so take it off, okay?"

She carefully stepped out of her dress and placed it to the side. Before she could step out of her shoes or slip or anything else he pounced, lifting her up and carrying her to the wall. He had already taken off his pants and put on protection in the time it took her to take off her dress and he had entered her just as quickly.

There was something about having the plaster wall at her back and the fully formed wall of muscle at her front that sent sexy, wanton chills up her spine. His hips moved forward deliberately and precisely. His movements caused him to hit spots in her that she hadn't even known existed.

"That dress is amazing, love. It's not my fault that we're gonna be late. That dress made me do this." He kissed her hard and long and she couldn't think.

She could only feel and it felt so darn good.

She bounced up and down his shaft, bounced on and off the wall, bounced from his right thigh to his left; she just bounced until she thought she might turn into a bouncing fool.

"Mmm… So no more dresses—"

"Oh, hell, yeah, more dresses! I can grow to love taking those things off you. In fact, tonight when we come home from the club, I'm taking it off you. And I promise I'll be gentle with it."

She melded her pelvis into his and ground down. She used the wall behind her as her base and proceeded to work him, moving her hips with gusto and zeal.

"That's right, love. Put it on me, girl." He thrust forward and gave as good as he got.

The frenzy they created must have been a sight to behold and she wished she could see them together. She was certain she would see that magic Patrick had been talking about a few months back when he was trying to convince her to go out on a date with him. In fact, as she felt herself tighten, release and explode, followed by his pulsing pumps and grunts of completion, she felt the magic for herself and her heart swelled.

When they finally made it to the supper club after a quick shower together and a quickie in the shower, she wasn't even sure she'd be able to dance the night away in Patrick's arms as she had planned. She was already pleasingly sore from his loving, even though the hot, steamy shower helped ease her aches a little.

All three of his brothers were already there with their wives, along with two other people she hadn't met yet. She would have thought that they were a couple, except that they were seated way across the table from one another.

The guy had the most intense hazel eyes she had ever seen. He had a golden-honeyed complexion and a megawatt smile. The woman had the most beautiful long black curls hanging down her back and Aisha figured she was Latina. Since Aisha was sitting by her, she figured she decided to introduce herself.

The woman seemed too busy glaring at the man at the other end of the table to pay much attention to Aisha's introduction, though.

"Oh, girl, I'm sorry. You feel so much like a part of the family already, I didn't realize you hadn't met my best friend, Maritza Morales, yet. She and my other best friend, Terrell, are visiting from California because little Jason Jr. has his christening tomorrow and they are the godparents." Penny smiled at Aisha. "So they were nice enough to give up their Valentine's Day plans and hang out with us the entire weekend. They're taking a much-needed break from each other right now, though, before someone gets hurt."

"Lovers' quarrel?" Aisha asked.

"Ooo…don't let her hear you say that. She will probably go off. They *technically* can't stand each other." Penny made quotation marks with her hand.

"Oh…" Aisha nodded, even though she didn't understand at all where Penny was going. Did the two people glowering at each other like each other or not? Were they a couple or not?

Oh, well, she couldn't be bothered. She turned to Patrick and he smiled at her.

He leaned over and whispered in her ear. "It's complicated when it comes to Terrell and Maritza. I'll explain it all to you later."

She nodded and smiled. This group certainly had its share of drama. She just hoped Valentine's Day wasn't nearly as exciting as Thanksgiving had been.

The food in the supper club was superb. It was nuevo soul and the chef had made all kinds of cool twists on traditional soul food favorites. They took a diaspora approach to the food and sampled flavors from all across the Caribbean and the African continent.

The couples had a private dining room and the appetizers, entrées and desserts had already been preselected. Everything was amazing, from the food to the company.

The décor was breathtaking, as well. The rich earth

tones of brown, green, rust, tan and orange were high-lighted with little pops and splashes of jewel tones from purple to emerald to ruby and topaz. A live jazz band played in the main dining room and the music was piped in, softly playing in the background of their room.

At first she didn't see how the evening was going to be romantic with so many couples. But the ambience was undeniable. And with the private room, it was almost as if they were having their own little Valentine's party.

And when they needed time alone, couples took to the small dance floor in the other room and moved to the jazz.

"Are you having a good time, Aisha? Feel like dancing a little?" Patrick reached over and covered her hand with his.

"I am stuffed. I need to dance for a little bit. How many courses did they serve us? Oh my God, that food was so-oo good. I'm gonna try that African peanut stew-style soup they served us. That was hearty."

"So I have an announcement, everyone." Maritza spoke to the group, but she seemed to be looking, or rather glaring, directly at Terrell as she tapped on her glass with her fork.

All the talking stopped and everyone looked at Maritza.

"As many of you know, I have been seeing Andrew 'Speedlo' Macgregor. And…well…he asked me to marry him yesterday and I've decided that I'm going to tell him yes." Maritza smiled, but it seemed very forced to Aisha.

"The white rapper, Speedlo?" Joel asked. Then he said, "Ouch" when Samantha elbowed him.

"You…ahh…you didn't say yes, right when he asked you?" Jason kept glancing back and forth between Maritza and Terrell.

Aisha leaned forward and glanced from one end of the table to the other, as well. Just when she thought there wasn't going to be any drama that evening, there appeared to be some brewing.

"No. He gave me the weekend to think it over. He knew I was coming to the christening and I wouldn't be in California on Valentine's Day, so—"

"So, seems that if you really wanted to marry him you would have said yes as soon as he asked. What's this you need to think? Either you love the man and want to marry him or you don't." Lawrence shook his head as he spoke and Aisha suddenly felt sorry for Maritza.

"Getting married is a big decision. Of course she wanted time to think it over before saying yes—" Aisha started and stopped when she got a poke from Patrick. "What?"

She looked at Patrick and he shook his head.

"Isn't Speedlo known for being kind of crazy? I mean *really* crazy. Half the lyrics on his first album had all this off-the-wall stuff about him wanting to kill his mother and his ex-wife. And you're saying you're gonna marry this guy?" Jason stared at Terrell as he spoke to Maritza.

"You ever heard of creative license, Jason? God. It's an act. He's not really crazy. He's really sweet." Maritza rolled her eyes. "You guys are worse than my brothers. I can just imagine what they're gonna say when I tell them."

"Well, I think it's wonderful. Love is a wonderful thing," Samantha said cheerfully.

"But does she love him?" Patrick asked, and it was Aisha's turn to poke him.

"Yeah. I can't wait. I know there will be all kinds of superstars at the wedding. I hope we're all invited." Minerva was fully showing now and she rubbed her medium-size baby bump as she spoke.

Penny, like Jason, just looked from Maritza to Terrell and seemed as if she wanted to say something, but said nothing instead.

Terrell got up and walked out of the room without saying a word and every eye in the room, including Maritza's, followed him out.

Drama! Carla was right. There never fails to be something popping off in this group.

Patrick clasped her hand. "Let's dance for a little bit."

She was torn between hanging out at the table to see what else happened and going to dance with the man she found herself increasingly growing to care for more than she was ready to admit.

Her need to be in Patrick's arms won out over her need to see how the drama unfolded, so she followed her man to the dance floor. Plus, she knew that Minerva and Samantha would have a blow-by-blow for her at the book club meeting.

She gently swayed to the mellow jazz music with

Patrick and she couldn't fight it anymore. It was just becoming harder and harder to try to hold back everything that she was coming to feel for him. So she just let herself feel it, even though she doubted that she would ever be able to voice it.

She stopped by the restroom on the way back to the private room and on her way out she heard angry voices just outside the women's restroom door. She listened carefully, because if it seemed like it was an abusive situation she was going to run and get the Hightower cops. She listened at the door for a minute to see if she needed to make a dash and get help.

It sounded like Maritza, at least the accent sounded like hers, and a man's voice she couldn't quite make out.

"You are not going to marry him and you know it, Maritza," the male voice snapped.

Yep, Maritza. I knew it.

"I am so going to marry him, Terrell. And it's none of your business anyway," Maritza hissed.

Hmm... Terrell. I probably should have guessed that one.

"You're not going to marry him because you love me, Maritza. And I'm done playing with you, girl. You're not marrying him."

Aw...sweet! I wonder what Maritza's going to say about that.

"I—" Maritza started.

The voices stopped and for a minute Aisha didn't hear anything. She leaned farther into the door but still heard nothing. After waiting a few minutes so that it didn't seem as if she were being rude and eavesdropping, she came out of the restroom and was shocked by what she saw.

Maritza and Terrell broke free from an embrace after what looked like a pretty hot and steamy kiss.

"Oh, sorry… Excuse me…" Aisha stumbled over her words. She certainly hadn't been expecting that at all.

Drama! I bet Maritza won't be marrying that Speedlo guy now. Not after the way she was liplocked with Terrell.

"You aren't marrying him, Maritza." Terrell gave her one more pointed stare and then left the two ladies standing there.

Aisha figured she'd make her awkward exit, but Maritza grabbed her arm.

"Please don't say anything to the others about what you saw. No matter what they all think, I am marrying Speedlo. So you can see why I wouldn't want this to get out."

Aisha just nodded at the woman. And went to find Patrick. She had a feeling that whatever was going on between Maritza and Terrell was far from over.

Drama!

Chapter 14

Her relationship with Patrick seemed solid; certainly more solid than any relationship she had ever had before. A month after the wonderful Valentine's Day weekend he'd arranged for her, she was still swooning. And even though she knew she needed to come down from cloud nine, she didn't want to. She just wanted to soak up as much of his caring and good loving as she possibly could. They had worked their way into a nice groove. When he had weekends off, he spent every single moment with her.

She was waiting for him to come back with some videos for their Saturday night in, when her ex showed up with Dillon a day early.

"I'm not going to babysit your brat while you screw

around with another man. And if you keep this up, I'm going to take my son out of this environment." Bill bit out his angry and bitter words.

She took a deep breath and remembered the pep talk that Patrick had given her about why she should give Bill and Dillon a chance to bond and Dillon a chance to get to know his father.

"You need to leave my home, Bill. I would feel more comfortable meeting you at a neutral and public space for drop-offs and pickups from now on if you're so determined to have your visitation rights. Even though we both know that my parents are doing more visiting with Dillon then you are anyway." She turned to her son. "How are Grandpa and Grandma these days, Dillon?"

Bill leaped toward her and shoved her against the wall. Pinned between the wall and Bill, she started to say her prayers that Patrick would hurry up and come back with the DVDs he'd gone out to rent.

"Get off her, Dad. Leave my mom alone!" Dillon latched on to Bill's leg and tried to pull him off.

Bill shoved Dillon away and then raised his hand and curled it into a fist. There was a knock at the door and a frightened Dillon answered the door without even asking who it was.

Luckily it was Patrick. Patrick pushed Bill off Aisha and flung him into the wall.

"Are you crazy, man? Don't you ever put your hands on her again! Is this the way you behave in front of your son?" Patrick spoke between clenched teeth as he grabbed Bill by the collar and shook him.

"Get your hands off me or I will sue you," Bill threatened as he tried to wiggle away from Patrick's grip.

Patrick lifted Bill with very little effort and tossed him out the front door. "If I ever... If I *ever* catch you with your hands on her again, you'll more than regret it!" Patrick slammed the door.

First he went to Dillon and checked him out. "Are you all right, little man? You okay?"

Dillon nodded his head, but Aisha could tell that her child was badly shaken.

She looked at her own hands and saw that they were shaking horribly, and she cursed herself. Why did she allow him to get to her like this?

"Love, are you okay? Did he hit you or hurt you at all?" Patrick checked her for bumps and bruises and pulled her into his arms. She pulled away and took deep breaths to calm herself.

"I'm okay." She shut her eyes and counted to ten, all the while telling herself to hold it together.

When she opened her eyes she plastered on a smile. "What do you say we get some Chinese takeout and rent another DVD, since Dillon is back to join in on our movie day? Dillon, the new ninja mutant spider movie is out. We can rent that." She walked over to her child and ruffled his hair.

Patrick eyed her cautiously and she could tell that even though she didn't have him fooled by a long shot, he was going to give her a pass.

Dillon nodded and the three of them left together to get food and rent movies.

The entire evening she had to make herself stay on top of her shaking hands. They were a definite tell that the altercation with Bill had gotten to her. And she didn't want to bother Patrick with all her drama.

She caught him glancing at her several times through dinner and the movie, even though she tried to keep it upbeat and take everyone's mind off what had happened.

Patrick was such a strong man and she wanted to be strong, too. She didn't like that he'd had to basically step in and save her from Bill. She felt as if she should have been able to save herself.

But how did she tell Patrick that? He probably wouldn't understand it. She barely understood it herself.

Once they put Dillon to bed, Patrick snuggled up to her and pulled her close to him in her bedroom.

"How are you feeling, love? Talk to me."

"I'm fine."

"You're not fine. I can tell." Patrick pulled her close. "It's okay to feel a little shaken up. It's okay to feel a little scared. I'm scared, too. I'm scared of what might have happened if I hadn't gotten here in time—"

"That's just it. I should have been able to handle it. I shouldn't have needed you to step in and get him off me. I never wanted my son to have to see that kind of crap. I should have been able to defend us better."

"Maybe you should get a restraining order on him, love. I'm thinking you need to have a safe drop-off spot for Dillon, too. Maybe you could drop Dillon off with your folks ahead of time and he can pick Dillon up from there after you leave. Dillon spends his visits there anyway." Patrick rubbed his hand over his face. She could see how worried he was for her, how much he cared.

"My father probably wouldn't agree to it. But I'll ask." She knew her father would side with his so-called son, Bill. But at that point she would have done anything to ease Patrick's worry. She owed him that much for stepping in and doing what she should have been able to do herself—protect herself and her child.

She sighed. "I don't want to talk about this anymore." She knew of other things they could do besides talk and she intended to do them until she wasn't afraid anymore. She needed to forget what had just happened. She needed Patrick to love away the hurt.

She straddled his hips and slowly began to take off his sweater. The thick, warm material felt good under her hands as she lifted it over his head and tossed it aside. But his skin felt even better.

Staring at him, she sucked her bottom lip as she contemplated what she would do next. His rippled chest with pectorals that looked like twin mounds of deep, dark chocolate called out to her. And she wanted to lick every muscle, examine every ridge.

But then there were the jeans he was wearing and what she knew awaited her once she got them off. Her fingers went to his buckle and she pulled off his belt. Once she got his pants unzipped and released him from the confines that held him, she stroked him until he grew large in her hands.

She eased down his chest, licking and sucking and nibbling the wall of muscle all the way until she reached his penis. She took him deep in her mouth and relished the salty, sweet taste of him.

"Oh... Love..." he groaned as he knotted his hands in her hair.

She took him deeper and found herself groaning, too.

Soon he lifted her and she reluctantly got up. He quickly undressed her and covered himself in protection. When he came back to the bed, she made him lie down on his back so that she could straddle him again.

As she lowered herself onto him, she could feel her muscles stretching and pulsing to fit him in. She loved the way he felt with her on top.

She lifted herself up and swirled her hips before dipping back down. She let her hands get their feel of the bold ridges of his chest before bending down and covering his mouth in a kiss. She pointed her tongue in an attempt to mimic the way he felt inside of her. She thrust into his mouth repeatedly, curving to touch the roof, bending to tangle with the tongue. She made a point of reaching every corner and crevice just as he seemed to be touching every part of her.

He cupped her behind and began to orchestrate her movements. He pulled her up and down his slick shaft with a precision matched only by his own moves in and out.

"You feel so good, Patrick. So... Good..."

Her back arched and she threw her head back, fighting the urge to scream because she knew her child was sleeping in the other room. She swallowed instead and moaned and sighed and moved, *always she moved.*

His hands could no longer contain her hips so he let go and cupped her breasts instead, holding them and gently stroking the nipples as they went up and down, up and down.

"What would it take to soundproof this room, love? I miss your screams…" He caught her nipple between his thumb and forefinger and squeezed gently as his buttocks lifted from the bed and he thrust powerfully. He had a seductive and slightly cocky smirk on his face.

Her eyes popped open and she groaned.

"You hear my screams all weekend and *every* time at your place." She pulled up, swirled and bounced back down. She got a rhythm going that kept her focused, on a mission. "Maybe I miss your screams, too…"

She worked him and soon his smirk disappeared.

"You don't look so good. You're not enjoying this?" she whispered as she pulled up, swirled and bounced.

"Don't… Okay… I give up… Uncle…" He moaned with a pleading and contrite expression on his face.

"Make that Auntie." Up. Swirl. Bounce. Down.

His eyes widened and he grabbed hold of her hips on the downstroke, holding her still as he made a powerful thrust upwards. He sat up as he pulled her closer, holding her and caressing her as he filled her almost impossibly full.

He planted a demanding and powerful kiss on her lips, forcing them open. And, as completion found them both, neither of them could scream. They shook in each other's arms and panted their release. Then he wrapped her in his arms and they both drifted off.

The last thing Aisha wanted was for him to go. But she didn't know if she were ready for her son to find a man waking up in their apartment. Even though they had been dating for a while, they only stayed the night at each other's places when Dillon was with his dad.

"Patrick, wake up, honey. You probably shouldn't stay the night. We don't want Dillon getting the wrong idea."

Patrick groaned, but he sat up and rubbed his face before looking at her. He seemed to study her for several minutes before he spoke.

"I don't feel good about leaving you. What if Bill comes back? I'd feel better if I was here with you."

"I think you scared him…for tonight anyway…. He won't be back. And you can't be here 24/7. So I'm going to have to learn how to handle Bill on my own at some point."

"Okay, love. But I just want you to know that I am serious about both you and Dillon and I want to be a permanent part of your lives." He reached out and cupped her chin, softly stroking her cheek with his thumb.

"Patrick, you see all the drama I have going on with my ex. We have such a long way to go before we can really start talking about permanence."

He shook his head. "Do you want to know why I have been calling you *love* since almost the very moment I met you?" He peered into her eyes and waited patiently for her answer.

"I don't know. I figured it was some guy thing. You know how you guys use *baby* and *queen* and *shorty* as the everywoman moniker so you won't slip up and mistakenly call someone the wrong name. Don't worry, I'm not mad at you, playa." She tried to lighten the mood with a joke, but he still wore his serious expression.

He shook his head. "No, love, that's not it by a long shot. I have called you *love* because that's what I felt from the first moment I set eyes on you. It caught me by surprise and I knew you weren't ready to hear that. You would have run for the hills and I would have never gotten that first date." He caressed her cheek again.

"But me being me, I had to verbalize it, I had to find a way to say what I felt, even if I couldn't actually tell you. I hope I've been showing you all this time, as well. But every time I called you *love* I've been telling you that I love you."

Her mouth dropped open. He couldn't really be serious, could he?

"I love you, Aisha, and that is permanent. I love you and I love Dillon." He kissed her on the forehead. "Sleep on that, love."

She got up and walked him to the door, knowing she would probably be up all night thinking about what Patrick had said to her.

Chapter 15

Aisha started a pot of chamomile tea, hoping it would relax her mind and help her go to sleep so that she could get some much-needed rest. Just as she sat down on the love seat with a blanket, her tea and this month's book club selection she heard a knock on the door.

"Who is it?" she asked. She looked through the peephole and saw Bill.

Oh. Hell. No.

She swallowed and her heart played the conga in her chest. She patted her chest to try to calm the beating, but it was no use. She nibbled at her lip and stepped back from the door.

"It's me. Open the door. We need to talk, okay? This is getting ridiculous."

She could hear the barely controlled anger in his voice and she tried to figure out the best words to use to try to get him to just go home and leave her alone. Her hand went to her neck as she thought about the way he had used a hold on her neck to slam her into the wall today. Just as she'd known when he'd punched her in the face that he would hit her again if she stayed. She knew that if she opened the door to talk to him he would use his hands and not his words.

She wished that Patrick were still there.

"Go home, Bill. I'm not letting you in here. Go home." She hated how shaky her voice sounded, despised the slight chatter in her teeth. But she was afraid.

He started pounding on the door and kicking it. Soon she saw the door rattling and moving and shaking. She knew it would be only a matter of time before he knocked the thing off the hinges.

Aisha ran into Dillon's bedroom and locked the door. She grabbed her sleeping child and they hid in the closet while she called the police and then Patrick on her cell phone.

Before she could finish telling Patrick what was going on, Bill had already made it into the apartment and was trying to break down Dillon's bedroom door.

Aisha kissed her son on the cheek. "Stay in the closet, sweetie, and don't come out no matter what. Okay, sweetie? Promise me, okay?"

Dillon alternated between nodding and shaking his head. "Okay, Mommy." He grabbed her arm. "Don't go, Mommy. Don't go."

"Here, sweetie, take Mommy's cell phone and use it in case the police or Patrick calls back, okay?" She tried to be strong and put up a front for her child. He was shaking and so was she. Her chest felt as if it was caving in and her throat was so dry her words croaked out. She figured she wasn't fooling anyone trying to be brave. But she had to try.

He continued to clutch her arm. But she loosened his fingers and left the closet to try to talk some sense into Bill.

Aisha stepped outside the door and put on as brave a face as she could. The fear from that afternoon hadn't left her, but she knew she had to be strong.

She took a deep, gulping breath and then another. "Bill, our son is sleeping and I would appreciate it if you would keep it down out here. I don't want you to wake him up."

Bill appeared more crazed than she had ever seen him. Before she could think better of her approach, he slapped her, knocking her to the floor.

"You don't get to tell me what to do, you stupid, pathetic little bitch. Do you think you're suddenly calling the shots because you're spreading your legs for a fireman?" He kicked her and she tried to scoot away and block his kicks by flailing her own legs out and trying to kick him.

He just kept kicking and hitting her and screaming foul names. She drowned out his hateful voice and the pain by thinking of Patrick.

Patrick, who was nothing like Bill; Patrick, whom she'd almost lost because she had let her fear control her.

Finally Bill stopped hitting her and started back toward Dillon's room. Her heart stopped. Her child. Not her child! She jumped up and grabbed his shirt to pull him back. Tears were falling down her face so hard she could barely see. But she couldn't let him get to Dillon. She just couldn't. Even if she couldn't protect herself, she would protect her child.

"I'm not leaving my son in this whorehouse." He made his move for Dillon's door again.

"You'll have to go through me. You'll have to kill me to take my son out of here!"

The sick, evil expression that crossed his face let her know that he would gladly do it.

"Are you okay, little man? Talk to me, Dillon." Patrick had never felt so much fear in his life and he never wanted to feel like this again.

"Yes. I'm fine. I'm just worried about my mom. He's loud. And he's hitting. I can tell by the sounds he's making. I want to go out and stop him." Dillon's voice sounded scared but brave.

Patrick knew the young boy would probably run out there to help. And he just didn't know if Bill would end up hurting both the mother and the child. Any man who would put his hands on a woman in anger was capable of anything, in Patrick's opinion.

"You stay put, Dillon. I'm on the way and my brothers, the police officers, are on their way, as well. Your mom would be really sad if something happened to you. You don't want to see her sad, do you?"

"No, I don't want her to be sad," Dillon whimpered. "But he's hurting her...."

Patrick broke every speed limit in the city and state, trying to make it to Aisha and Dillon. The guilt he felt for leaving them alone and vulnerable threatened to overwhelm him.

She lived only a few blocks away from him, but it seemed like hundreds as he raced to get there. He knew both of his police detective brothers were also on their way, along with other police officers. But he also knew that these kinds of domestic violence situations, where the abused spouse had left and moved on, often ended up with the woman dead because the abuser refused to leave the woman alone to be free and happy.

Even though Patrick was trying to keep a calm and soothing voice and tone for the scared little boy he had come to think of as his own son, he couldn't help but worry that he and his brothers might get there too late.

Aisha knew the last thing she could do was let Bill go into Dillon's room.

What would a sick abuser like Bill do, once he realized he could no longer control her with her fear for her own well-being? He would try to hurt her child. She knew he would, because he knew she cared more for her child than for anything else.

She grabbed hold of his arm and refused to let him go. She had no idea she could grip anything so tightly. She tried her best to pull him away, but she managed only baby steps.

Bill laughed his ugly, harsh, hateful laugh and gave her one of his leering gazes. "What are you willing to do to save your little brat? You willing to spread them for me like you spread them for that fireman?"

Her grip loosened slightly and he snatched his arm away.

The thought of having Bill ever touch her in that way again sickened her to her core.

After knowing what real love and caring felt like in Patrick's arms, she knew she would rather die than let Bill get close to her intimately again.

Just as his disgusting, creepy hand reached out and cupped her breast, he was snatched back and placed in handcuffs. Lawrence Hightower threw Bill against the wall and Jason read him his Miranda rights. Two uniformed police officers were also with the Hightower detectives.

When Patrick appeared seconds later, it took all four of the other men to keep him off Bill. Even with them holding him, he got off two solid punches to Bill's jaw.

"Dammit, Patrick, chill. You don't want this fool to get off on a technicality," Jason said and he pulled his brother away.

"And we don't want to have to take you in for assault. This lowlife isn't worth it. Go see about your woman and her child," Lawrence stated.

Aisha felt numb and weary, but at least she had kept that monster away from her child.

The uniformed officers took Bill away, and Jason and Lawrence took her statement while Patrick comforted Dillon.

The bruises and blood on Aisha horrified Patrick. It took everything in him, every single nurturing instinct that he didn't even know he had, to remain calm while he rocked the scared Dillon to sleep.

"Thank you, God, for keeping him safe." Patrick threw his head to the sky and whispered a prayer.

He only wished that he could have just a few minutes alone with the bastard. Once he put Dillon to sleep, he went back into the living room to check on Aisha.

"Thank you so much, Lawrence and Jason, for getting here when you did. I don't know what I would have done without my cop brothers. No more firemen-are-better-than-cop jokes for a month at least."

"It's all good, Patrick. Just take care of her and Dillon We'll catch you later." Jason gave him a hug.

"Love you, man. Keep them safe." Lawrence hugged him, too, and they both left.

Aisha went to the bathroom to wash her face and check out her bruises.

Patrick followed her to the bathroom. "Maybe we should take you to the hospital and have a doctor check you out."

"I'm fine."

"We need to take photographs of the bruises. We'll need them to build a case against him. Documenting what he did, along with the police report, should help get a restraining order and get his visitation rights revoked."

He would have felt better if she had gone to the hospital, but he didn't push it. He could tell she was trying to put on a brave face, and that made him love her all the more.

"I have a camera in the hall closet."

He got the camera, then proceeded to take pictures of each and every bruise. As they stood in the bathroom and he photographed the bruises on her face, back and arms, his anger boiled and his heart ached with each one. He had never felt so helpless in his life. What he wanted to do he knew he couldn't, or else he'd be in jail and useless to Aisha and Dillon.

He knew there was no way he could go on the way they had been going. The courtship was taking too long. He had found his family and he wanted them—his future wife and son—now.

Wrapping his arm around Aisha, he led her to the living room and they sat for a while in silence. All he did was hold her.

She began to cry and he let her get it out. Each tear she shed made him want to cry himself, or, preferably, kill Bill Miller.

When she had spent all her tears, Patrick pulled her tightly to him. "Look at me, love."

Her red, blurry eyes were swollen and one seemed as if it was getting the beginnings of a black eye, but she still looked like the picture of beauty to him.

"I love you. I don't want to spend one more moment without you. Please, love, take a chance on love just one more time and be my wife." He rocked her slowly in his arms and felt the tears falling down his cheeks.

She couldn't believe that he had actually asked her to marry him. She knew without a doubt that she loved him. But marriage seemed like something a long way away. Something for when they had been dating a long enough time...

"I love you, too, Patrick. But maybe we should just take it slow—"

"Love, that's not an option. Believe me when I say I don't want to pressure you, especially not now after what you've just been through. But I have plans for you, me, Dillon and the little brothers and sisters we're going to give him." He brushed his lips softly across her swollen ones. "I'm not leaving tonight. I'm not leaving the two of you unprotected *ever* again. Marry me, love. Marry me."

Aisha exhaled and let everything he said swirl around in her head. She looked him in the eye and saw the love he had for her flowing. Just that sweet, tender look from him let her know that he was serious.

She thought about her feelings, the ones she'd been trying to hold back from the moment she first saw him and he came barreling into her life, refusing to take no for an answer and talking about just wanting to get to know her.

She exhaled. "I'm so glad that one of us was brave enough to believe in magic and go after what we could be together. Thank you, Patrick, for loving me enough to make me see it, for waiting for me to catch up. I love you." She caressed his face, savoring his mahogany-brown handsomeness.

"Will you marry me?"

"I'll marry you, Patrick. I'd be honored to be your wife."

He leaned forward and gently brushed her lips. She might have been a little bruised by Bill's beating, but she wasn't broken or bowed.

She was loved and she was finally brave enough to reach out and grab all the love her heart could carry. All the love the sexy fire captain was waiting to give her....

After spending the night being held by Patrick in his strong, loving arms, Aisha felt rejuvenated. She didn't let the black-and-blue marks on her face and body sway her. Her heart was full of love for her son and her man, and that give her strength. She felt good and she felt like making breakfast for the two amazing men in her life.

Gently unraveling herself from Patrick's arms, she went into the kitchen and turned the CD player to Mary J. Blige's "Just Fine." She practiced her dance moves as she mixed and poured the pancake batter.

She didn't even have to go back and wake the two of them. First Patrick came out in his jeans and no shirt. She let her eyes linger on his chiseled form and thanked the Almighty that she hadn't succeeded in turning this gift of a man away. If she hadn't been so busy with the pancakes, she might have given in to the urge to rub her hands down those ripples, to give those muscular arms a squeeze. As she started to consider doing just that, Dillon came out in his super ninja spider pajamas.

"Hey, guys, I made some pancakes. So I hope you're hungry." She smiled at them.

"Well, that depends, Mom. Are these the regular pancakes from the box, or are they a recipe you got off the TV?" Dillon asked after clearing his throat.

"They smell heavenly, love. But I'm with Dillon… Regular or concoction?" Patrick gave her one of his devilish grins.

She put her hand on her hip and gave them the most menacing look she could, especially since she wanted to burst out laughing at their antics.

"They're just plain ol' pancakes, guys. I followed the directions on the box to the letter and didn't add a thing. I didn't get the idea or half of the recipe from watching any TV cooking show, so help me God." She put her hand up in the scout's-honor pose. "So if you guys don't want these to get cold, then you need to sit down."

She took out the pancakes she was keeping warm in the oven and added the new batch to the platter. She also took the syrup out of the microwave and set everything on the table.

Patrick and Dillon started filling up their plates with gusto and soon Dillon was covering his pancakes with the warm syrup. Seeing him pour so much on his pancakes gave her a moment of pause.

"Um…I did get this idea from Paula's show about the syrup where you put some—"

"Oh, brother… M-o-m… What did you do to the syrup? What's wrong with plain old Mrs. Butterworth's?"

"I just wanted to try something new. You might actually like it, you know. She said to use fresh cinnamon and a little fresh lemon and orange zest, but I didn't have any fresh cinnamon or oranges or lemons so I improvised. But I'm sure it will be good."

Patrick shook his head and chuckled. He switched his unsyrup-covered pancakes for Dillon's plate, went over to the counter and got the regular syrup bottle for Dillon. He sat down in front of the syrup-covered pancakes and winked at her before saying a quick prayer and digging in.

"I'll eat your concoctions, love. You know this means you have to stay with me for the rest of your life."

She giggled. "It means you love me and I love you." She leaned over and placed a soft kiss on his lips.

"And don't you ever doubt it, love," Patrick said as he caressed her bruised face.

She might have looked frightening, with all the black-and-blue marks. But she was the most beautiful woman in the world in Patrick's eyes.

"Oh, brother…" Dillon said in between bites of his pancakes. "You two are *really* sappy."

She mussed her son's curly hair and made the sappiest face she could. "Don't worry, we love you to pieces, too, my little sweetie."

"M-o-m…" Dillon gave Patrick a pleading glance and Patrick put on his best sappy-faced expression.

"Your mom is right, Dillon. We love you very, very much."

Both she and Dillon burst out laughing when they looked at Patrick, and soon they were all cracking up and enjoying one another.

That happy family feeling came over her again and this time she relished it. She let it wash away all the pain and hurt because she knew that it was going to last.

Epilogue

Two years later

"Come here, son. Let me help you fix your tie."

Patrick straightened Dillon's tie with a look of love and pride on his face,

The twelve-year-old young man stood still, all the while shaking his head. "Dad, I don't know who's worse—you or Mom."

Patrick chuckled. "Oh, that's easy. Your mom is worse."

"What did you say?" Aisha finally finished getting their daughter, Chloe, out of the car seat and walked over to them with the baby in her arms.

They had been married a little under two years and

had welcomed the newest addition to their family a year ago today.

Chloe Elizabeth Hightower's christening was today and Patrick was happier than he had ever known he could be.

"What am I supposedly worse about this time?" Aisha asked their son.

That was another thing he would never get tired of saying. *Their son.* Ever since Bill had decided to give up his rights to Dillon, following a last-ditch effort to try to hurt Aisha, Patrick had hurried to make legal what he had always felt in his heart. Dillon was completely his now. He was a Hightower.

"Babying me. I'm twelve now, you guys. I'm a preteen. Y'all are going to have to stop with the babying." Dillon grinned through his mock-serious expression.

"You'll always be my baby," Aisha said with a smile as she handed Chloe to Patrick.

Patrick took his daughter as he drank in his wife, son and beautiful baby girl with his eyes.

"Love…"

His wife turned and gazed at him with her beautiful brown-sugar eyes.

"Yes?"

"Thank you for giving me the most amazing family a man could ever hope for. I love you."

"I love you, too."

They walked into the church, surrounded by family and friends, and it felt amazing. Everyone was there. All his brothers, their wives and children, his parents. His aunt Sophie had even made her amends and was slowly making her way back into the family. She'd said she wouldn't miss her grandniece's christening for anything in the world. Even Carla and Gerald had showed up.

"Everyone's here...except my mom...." Aisha's happy face took on a slight sadness. She had cut her father out of her life and didn't expect that to ever change.

Patrick couldn't believe that her father still took Bill's side after what he'd done to her, and that he'd even represented Bill in the criminal case. But he knew she still held out hope that one day her mom would come around.

"Of course everyone is here, love. This was what it was all about at the end of the day. Family, honor, loyalty, but most important of all, love."

Aisha gazed at her husband and their children. She loved the way he had stepped in and become the father that her son needed. She loved that he fought to make it legal and binding so that Dillon would never have to worry about being wanted or loved again. She just loved the man because he had been patient enough to wait for her to realize that they could be magic together. And she felt the sudden urge to give him the gift she'd been keeping secret for the past two days.

"Patrick," she said softly, "I'm pregnant."

"Yes!" Dillon pumped his fist. "This time it has to be a boy!"

"Boy or girl is fine with me. I'm just happy you finally said yes," Patrick offered in his most heartfelt voice. He covered Aisha's mouth with a deep kiss and all she could do was agree with him.

* * * * *

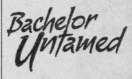

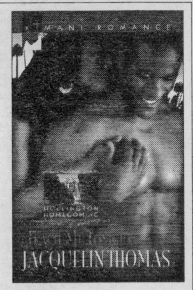

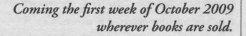

REQUEST YOUR FREE BOOKS!

2 FREE NOVELS
PLUS 2 FREE GIFTS!

KIMANI ROMANCE™

Love's ultimate destination!

KROM09

HELP CELEBRATE
ARABESQUE'S
15TH ANNIVERSARY!

ARABESQUE®

2009 marks Arabesque's 15th anniversary!

Help us celebrate by telling us about your most special memories and moments with Arabesque books. Entries will be judged by the Arabesque Anniversary Committee based on which are the most touching and well written. Fifteen lucky winners will receive as a prize a full-grain leather duffel bag with the Arabesque anniversary logo.

How to Enter: To enter, hand-print (or type) on an 8 ½" x 11" plain piece of paper your full name, mailing address, telephone number and a description of your most special memories and moments with Arabesque books (in two hundred [200] words or less) and send it to "Arabesque 15th Anniversary Contest 20901"—in the U.S.: Kimani Press, 233 Broadway, Suite 1001, New York, NY 10279, or in Canada: 225 Duncan Mill Road, Don Mills, ON M3B 3K9. No other method of entry will be accepted. The contest begins on July 1, 2009, and ends on December 31, 2009. Entries must be postmarked by December 31, 2009, and received by January 8, 2010. A copy of these Official Rules is available online at www.myspace.com/kimanipress, or to obtain a copy of these Official Rules (prior to November 30, 2009), send a self-addressed, stamped envelope (postage not required from residents of VT) to "Arabesque 15th Anniversary Contest 20901 Rules," 225 Duncan Mill Road, Don Mills, ON M3B 3K9. Limit one (1) entry per person. If more than one (1) entry is received from the same person, only the first eligible entry submitted will be considered. By entering the contest, entrants agree to be bound by these Official Rules and the decisions of Harlequin Enterprises Limited (the "Sponsor"), which are final and binding.

NO PURCHASE NECESSARY. Open to legal residents of U.S. and Canada (except Quebec) who have reached the age of majority at time of entry. Void where prohibited by law. Approximate retail value of each prize: $131.00 (USD).

VISIT **WWW.MYSPACE.COM/KIMANIPRESS**
FOR THE COMPLETE OFFICIAL RULES

KPI15ARACONTEST